STAR TREK®
STARFLEET ACADEMY®

4/4

#3: ***CADET KIRK***

DIANE CAREY

Interior illustrations by
Todd Cameron Hamilton

A
MINSTREL®
BOOK

Published by POCKET BOOKS
New York   London   Toronto   Sydney   Tokyo   Singapore

A MINSTREL PAPERBACK *Original*

 A Minstrel Book published by
POCKET BOOKS, a division of Simon & Schuster Inc.
1230 Avenue of the Americas, New York, NY 10020

Copyright © 1996 by Paramount Pictures. All Rights Reserved.

 STAR TREK is a Registered Trademark of
A VIACOM COMPANY Paramount Pictures.

This book is published by Pocket Books, a division of Simon & Schuster Inc., under exclusive license from Paramount Pictures.

ISBN: 0-671-00077-2

First Minstrel Books printing October 1996

10 9 8 7 6 5 4 3 2 1

A MINSTREL BOOK and colophon are registered trademarks of Simon & Schuster Inc.

Printed in the U.S.A.

*Dedicated to the children of the men and women of
the United States Armed Forces*

STARFLEET TIMELINE

1969   Neil Armstrong walks on Earth's moon.

2156   Romulan Wars begin between Earth forces and the Romulan Star Empire.

2160   Romulan peace treaty signed, establishing the Neutral Zone.

2161   United Federation of Planets formed; Starfleet established with charter "to boldly go where no man has gone before."

2218   First contact with the Klingon Empire.

2245   Starship *U.S.S. Enterprise* NCC-1701 launched on its first five-year mission under the command of Captain Robert April and First Officer Christopher Pike.

2249   Spock enters Starfleet Academy as the first Vulcan student. Leonard McCoy enters Starfleet Medical School.

2250   James T. Kirk enters Starfleet Academy.

2251   Christopher Pike assumes command of the *Enterprise* for its second five-year mission.

2252 Spock, still a Starfleet cadet, begins serving under Captain Pike on the *Enterprise*.

2253 Spock graduates from Starfleet Academy. Leonard McCoy graduates from Starfleet Medical School.

2254 James T. Kirk graduates from Starfleet Academy. As a lieutenant, Kirk is assigned duty aboard the *U.S.S. Farragut*.

2261 *U.S.S. Enterprise*, under the command of Captain Christopher Pike, completes its third five-year mission.

2263 James T. Kirk is promoted to captain of the *Enterprise* and meets Christopher Pike, who is promoted to fleet captain.

2264 Captain James T. Kirk, in command of the *U.S.S. Enterprise*, embarks on a historic five-year mission of exploration.

2266 Dr. Leonard McCoy replaces Dr. Mark Piper as chief medical officer aboard the *Enterprise*.

2269 Kirk's original five-year mission ends, and Starship *Enterprise* returns to spacedock. Kirk is promoted to admiral.

2271   *U.S.S. Enterprise* embarks on Kirk's second five-year mission (*Star Trek: The Motion Picture*).

2277   James T. Kirk accepts a teaching position at Starfleet Academy; Spock assumes command of the Starship *Enterprise*.

2285   In orbit around the Genesis planet, Kirk orders the destruction of the Starship *Enterprise* to prevent the ship from falling into Klingon hands (*Star Trek III: The Search for Spock*).

2286   Kirk is demoted to captain and assigned command of the Starship *Enterprise* NCC-1701-A (*Star Trek IV: The Voyage Home*).

2287   The *Enterprise* is commandeered by Sybok, Spock's half-brother, and taken to the center of the galaxy (*Star Trek V: The Final Frontier*).

2292   Alliance between the Klingon Empire and the Romulan Star Empire collapses.

2293   The Klingon Empire launches a major peace initiative; the crews of the *U.S.S. Enterprise* and the *U.S.S. Excelsior*, captained by Hikaru Sulu, thwart a conspiracy to sabotage the Khitomer Peace Conference. Afterward, the *Enterprise-A* is decommissioned, and Kirk retires from Starfleet.

U.S.S. Enterprise NCC-1701-B, under the command of Captain John Harriman, is severely damaged on her maiden voyage. Honored guest Captain James T. Kirk is listed as missing, presumed killed in action.

2344 *U.S.S. Enterprise* NCC-1701-C, under the command of Captain Rachel Garrett, is destroyed while defending the Klingon outpost on Narendra III from Romulan attack.

2346 Romulan massacre of Klingon outpost on Khitomer.

2364 Captain Jean-Luc Picard assumes command of the *U.S.S. Enterprise* NCC-1701-D.

2367 Borg attack at Wolf 359; *U.S.S. Saratoga* destroyed; First Officer Lieutenant Commander Benjamin Sisko and his son, Jake, are among the survivors; *Enterprise* defeats the Borg vessel in orbit around Earth.

2369 Commander Benjamin Sisko assumes command of Deep Space Nine in orbit over Bajor.

2371 *U.S.S. Enterprise* NCC-1701-D destroyed on Veridian III.

Former *Enterprise* captain James T. Kirk emerges from a temporal nexus, but dies helping Picard save the Veridian system.

U.S.S. Voyager, under the command of Captain Kathryn Janeway, is accidentally transported to the Delta Quadrant. The crew begins a 70-year journey back to Federation space.

2372 The Klingon Empire's attempted invasion of Cardassia Prime results in the dissolution of the Khitomer peace treaty between the Federation and the Klingon Empire.

Source: *Star Trek® Chronology* / Michael Okuda and Denise Okuda

CADET KIRK

Chapter 1

"This is the coldest loading bay I've ever been in! I hope that bucket has heat inside, because I'm losing the feeling in my toes. Is that the door? You're in my way, kid."

This was one of *those* days. The annoying kind. The kind when nothing went wrong, exactly, but a hundred little tiny things didn't go right.

Like at this moment, there was a hole in Leonard McCoy's left shoe. He'd gotten dressed in the dark this morning because his eyes were tired. That was because he stayed up too late last night studying for an exam on the Orion respiratory system, and he'd accidentally put on an old pair of shoes that he had intended to throw away.

Now they were on McCoy's feet. Every time he took a step, cold air was sucked into that hole, blasting the side of his foot.

And there, in the middle of the loading bay, was the *Zodiac*-class warp shuttle, all warmed up. He was finally going to be able to settle down in a quiet, *warm* vehicle and read a book.

But there was something in his way.

The uniformed individual he'd just asked to move aside.

McCoy noticed the kid's face—fair-skinned, with a touch of outdoor ruddiness, topped by buff-colored hair. The hazel-eyed teenager wore the typical tinsel-gray shirt of a Starfleet Academy student. The traditional color had been around almost a hundred years, and was meant to imitate the shimmer of water off Point Bonita Light at the entrance of San Francisco Bay. The fabric had been chosen by one of the first Starfleet admirals, inspired as he looked out over the Bay past the 1877 lighthouse. That was when they had decided to locate Starfleet Command and the Academy in San Francisco.

The younger fellow didn't seem impressed by McCoy's gruff attitude. "I'm not a kid, sir," the kid said. "I'm a cadet."

McCoy nodded briskly. "Good for you. Pardon me."

But the cadet stayed in the way. "Sorry. Regulations say you can't board any Starfleet vessel without proper authorization."

"Starfleet vessel!" McCoy looked at the scout ship.

It was a banged-up box with two sausage-shaped impulse engines running the whole length of the hull and extending beyond the small crew compartment. On a vessel this small, the hyperlight engine system made up almost half the craft's weight. It was hardly a "Starfleet vessel" in the way this kid was referring to it.

2

"What do you mean I can't board?" McCoy demanded. He palmed his brown hair back and wished he'd gotten a haircut yesterday.

"You're not allowed to go on board. That's the rule, sir."

"Look, strong-arm, have you given any thought to why that rule exists?"

"No, sir."

"That code is to keep people from wandering onto ships of the line and full-sized transports, not two-ton taxicabs, Corporal."

"That's not what it says, sir. It says 'any' Starfleet vessel. And I'm a *cadet,* sir."

"But you're supposed to pick me up!"

The cadet's jaw tightened. "I have my passenger manifest. Your name's not on it. Regulations say you can't get on this shuttle without authorization. Nobody but a flight officer can change that without signed orders from Starfleet Central Dispatch. I haven't received any order countermanding my manifest."

McCoy stepped to one side and waved his arm toward the distant control offices. "All you have to do is walk across the bay to that communications station over there. Contact Central Dispatch and verify the change in your orders. How about that?"

"I'm not allowed to leave my ship, sir."

"Not allowed—*your* ship?" The medic tried to keep the blood running in his cold legs and feet. "How 'bout if I stand guard while you go over there and contact Dispatch?"

"You're not authorized to do that, sir."

3

Stiffening, McCoy pulled at his shirt. "What do you think this rag is? I'm a Starfleet ensign."

"Medical Corps, sir. Only Starfleet flight-certified officers can countermand the orders of—"

"Yes," McCoy interrupted, "but I outrank you."

The feisty cadet raised his chin. "You can certainly order me around," he said, and cocked his head toward the warp shuttle. "But you can't order the ship around."

Staring, McCoy leaned forward. "Are you saying I've got to have a blessing from Starfleet Command to stand next to a box with an engine on it while you walk across the loading bay?"

"That's right."

"Look, Generalissimo, I don't want to stand out here—*freezing*—until you find a regulation you like. Something's got to give."

"Yes, sir, as soon as the person arrives who *is* on the manifest. We'll see if he brings any changes in orders for me."

"Listen, junior!" McCoy blurted. "It's freezing out here! I was told to come to this bay and pick up this dogsled, right here, on this dock. I'm getting on board before I have to test for my medical license by amputating my own toes. Stand aside."

McCoy tucked his chin and took three steps up the stumpy boarding ramp, heading for the open hatchway. He could hear the heater whirring inside.

But suddenly the cadet jumped up onto the top of the ramp, a clean three-foot hop. "I'd rather not have to prevent you from doing so, sir," he said flatly, being careful of his tone.

He stood with legs braced, blocking the hatchway.

4

The country boy in Leonard McCoy made him think about duking it out with this cocky kid, because that was how a lot of folks handled things back in Georgia, where he came from.

On the other hand, a lot of people back there needed medical care. He'd spent his younger days patching together the bruised and broken parts of other kids in his neighborhood. Now he was a medical intern, on his way toward becoming a doctor.

He gazed up the ramp at the stocky body and muscular thighs and arms of the younger fellow, elbows slightly bent. The kid had a wrestler's body, compact and strong, and eyes like amber tigers staring out of the dark grass.

McCoy started to think he might be smarter *not* to have to patch himself together.

With most of his weight on his aching foot, he held still for a moment. "I'd . . . rather you didn't have to either. Maybe I'll just stand out here in the nice cold bay. . . ."

"Good idea, sir."

McCoy backed down the ramp. The cadet didn't move until the medic cleared the ramp.

Then he got off too.

"So,"McCoy attempted, "when *do* you think the iron gate might go up and I could get on board?"

"As soon as the person who is supposed to be transported gets here. Then we'll see if the manifest has been amended."

"I guess I'll wait."

"I guess you will." The cadet turned his back and attended to something inside an open mechanics hatch.

No matter how much McCoy stared in blustering

anger at the spot right between the boy's shoulder blades, the cadet refused to note that he was being stared at.

What a snot! the medic thought. This was one of those military types who not only followed rules, but actually *liked* them. Probably came from a long line of soldiers. Could probably quote the rank, regiment, and serial number of his great-great-great-grandfather from the Light Brigade.

Ah-hah! Somebody was coming through the access tunnel from the main terminal. He could see a narrow form walking their way, cast in shadows inside the tunnel. Finally!

He kept his eyes on the lean form striding toward them. Narrow shoulders, long legs, no hat, but maybe a helmet, the newcomer stepped into the bright lights of the loading dock.

A Vulcan! And not just any Vulcan, either—this was a Vulcan he knew!—*Spock!* What luck!

Oh, this trip is going to be fun, fun, fun. He clapped his hands and rubbed them. He started polishing his wooden-man jokes as he watched the young alien scientist approach. Like McCoy, the Vulcan was dressed in a typical Alaska-silver Starfleet Academy uniform shirt. His black hair was cut in a helmet shape that had fooled McCoy under those shadows a moment ago, but now caught the loading lights in a single bright band.

How strange it still was to see a Vulcan in a Starfleet uniform. Ensign Spock was the first Vulcan to choose Starfleet Academy over the Vulcan Science Academy, even after receiving scholarships to both. He was the first scientist to leave Vulcan for Starfleet. McCoy knew

Vulcans kept pretty much to themselves. They were content to spend their lives in study, preferring fact over philosophy, sticking close to the hard sciences.

Just perfect for picking on.

Maybe this wasn't going to be such a boring trip after all.

McCoy called across the loading bay. "Ensign Spock! How charming and inspiring to see you again. You're looking as chipper as ever—I'm glad you're here."

"Ensign McCoy . . . are you going to Colony Cambria for the Starfleet Academy Science Conference?"

"That's right. Medical Division seminars on the effects of life in space and on alien worlds. You know the type of place I mean . . . hot, dry, thin air, not enough moisture for a camel, places where no living thing was ever meant to live—oh, yes, I forgot. Vulcan's a little like that, isn't it?"

The young Vulcan paused and frowned at him. "In some regions. Have you cleared with Starfleet Dispatch?"

"Yes, I have. I was told to report to this shuttle, because it's scheduled to go there anyway, so I wouldn't have to wait for a regular Federation transport, but Corporal Goose-step over there wouldn't let me on board. Something about regulations."

"Cadet, not Corporal." Ensign Spock looked at the young man who silently waited for them. The cadet matched Spock's stony face with his own.

Spock drew his pin-straight brows together. His mushroom complexion and triangular features were etched by the bright dock lights as if drawn in sharp pencil.

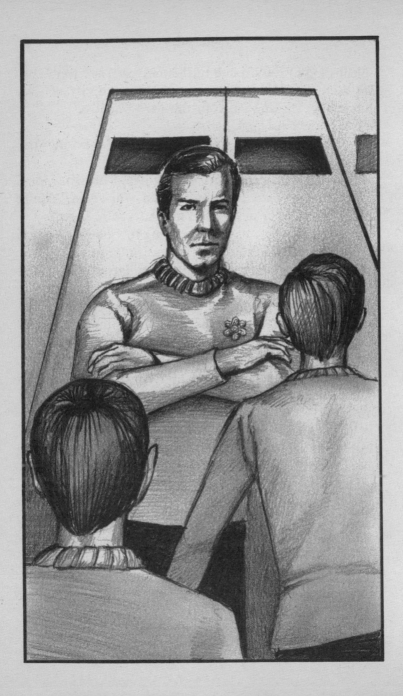

"I am Ensign Spock," he said. "Specify the point of contention, please, Cadet."

The cadet stepped forward. "Sir, the Starfleet Transport Code specifies that no one shall board a fueled Fleet warp vessel without specific confirmation from Central Dispatch."

"But I *do* have confirmation!" McCoy insisted.

Spock looked at him. "What is the code number on your authorization to take this scout?"

Glaring back at him, McCoy said, "I didn't memorize it!"

Unimpressed, Spock turned away from him and back to the pilot. "Good work, Cadet."

"Thank you, sir."

Ignoring the infuriated medic behind him, Spock stepped to the young man and held out a leather pouch. "This is your new flight order packet. You are to depart immediately for Colony Cambria, with myself and Ensign McCoy as your passengers. You are to follow your regularly scheduled flight route, including all scheduled stops."

Spock stepped past the cadet. McCoy followed him closely, determined to get on board that nice warm vehicle even if he had to do it with a Vulcan as his guard. He cast the kid a so-there glower as he passed him.

But the cadet followed them, got in front, and once again blocked the way.

"Sir," the cadet said, raising his voice, "I protest."

Turning to the seventeen-year-old, Spock crooked an eyebrow at him. "I beg your pardon?"

"I protest, sir." The cadet went to even stiffer attention. "I have my assignment, and, respectfully, you are not it."

Squaring off with the boy, Ensign Spock was suddenly more imposing than he first appeared. "Are you defying this change in orders?"

"If necessary, sir."

"What is your name?"

"Cadet Kirk, sir. And until I'm officially informed of a change in plans by Starfleet Dispatch, this warp shuttle isn't leaving here."

Chapter 2

"Explain that immediately," the Vulcan ordered.

The fiery young cadet obviously didn't like having to talk back to someone who outranked him—although he hadn't had much trouble talking back to McCoy. Evidently he wasn't impressed by medics, but the senior-ranking scientist bothered him.

And Vulcans had that naturally intimidating manner about them.

"Sir," the cadet insisted, "I know who my passenger is supposed to be . . . and neither of you is he. I'm supposed to be transporting the keynote speaker to the conference."

The Vulcan tipped his head as if he wasn't sure he heard right. "You were supposed to transport Dr. Richard Daystrom? Head of the United Federation of Planets Computer Science Department? In *this* craft?"

"The *Spitfire* is the biggest warp craft I'm rated to fly, sir."

McCoy stepped between them. "And Dr. Richard Daystrom, the most famous computer genius of our time, is supposed to get on this boat so you can drive him around? How did that happen!"

The cadet's chalk-mark eyebrows shot together. "I got top grades in all my subjects. I gave up my weekends. I scored highest in the preflight tests for warp rating. This is my . . ."

He stopped, suddenly uneasy in front of them, especially the Vulcan, who obviously wasn't impressed.

"Reward?" McCoy filled in.

"Well . . . yes. Only one cadet every semester gets this. There isn't supposed to be anybody on board but Dr. Daystrom and his assistant. I'm supposed to take him to the colony, then escort him around. It's going to be in all the news. Until I'm officially informed of a change, I'm going to resist leaving here."

Ensign Spock's voice was crisp, his black eyes were severe. "Cadet, you *are* being informed. *I* am informing you. Check the orders packet."

The cadet shifted his eyes to the leather pouch and opened it. Silently and unhappily he read it. He paced off a few steps. His permanent position of "attention" lost some of its stiffness.

"Well?" Spock clasped his hands behind his back.

Cadet Kirk hesitantly faced them again. Red-faced and white-knuckled, his face grim, he shoved the orders back into the packet. "Dr. Daystrom has been detained several hours. I'm supposed to take you to the colony, then wait there for further orders."

1 2

He seemed to feel he'd been cheated. His anger showed plainly. He wouldn't be opening the door for the famous Dr. Daystrom. He wouldn't be in the news tomorrow.

Shoving the packet against Spock's chest, the cadet stepped past them both and snapped, "Permission to board."

The *Spitfire* hummed with energy. Its impulse engines powered up for the ride out of the solar system. Waiting quietly in back were the warp engines, which would allow the little craft to jump beyond the speed of light and go very far indeed.

After leaving the loading dock, the small vessel hovered outside of Starbase One's giant turning spool of metal and lights. They were waiting for clearance to depart from the solar system.

Warp travel had been used for almost a century, but it was still somewhat of a technical marvel. Some aspects of technology used by Starfleet still made McCoy nervous. He wasn't quite ready to trust some of the contraptions that others took for granted.

Suspicious that this Cadet Kirk was all steam and no thrust, McCoy slipped forward to the cockpit and stuck his head in. "Is there a regulation against my sitting up here?"

"None that I know of," Cadet Kirk said frostily. He sat like a ramrod in the pilot's seat. He implied that if there were such a regulation, he'd use it to keep away from the two passengers who had ruined his reward. He touched the communications grid.

"This is Starfleet Zodiac *Spitfire,* nine-one-six Delta

India Yankee, departing for Colony Cambria, standard spaceways. Will make contact with Junction Buoy two-nine-nine-three in the Agira Basin. ETA is zero eight hundred thirty hours . . . mark. Request clearance to depart."

From Starfleet Flight Control, a gravelly voice chipped back over the comm signal. *"Zodiac nine-one-six Delta India Yankee, this is the dockmaster. You're cleared for launch on spacelane Charlie Four, Vector Twenty-five, no-wake speed."*

"Roger that."

McCoy sat down in the copilot's seat. "What does that mean?"

"It's our angle of takeoff out of the solar system. So we don't hit anybody else coming or going from Earth."

"What's 'no-wake'?"

"It's an old term that came up from days of steamships and engine-driven vessels on water. It means going slow enough that you don't disturb other vessels. In this case, slowly enough to turn or stop quickly. There are lots of other vessels coming and going. We have to be careful not to hit any of them." Cadet Kirk pinched his lips together. "You a doctor?"

"I'm a medic. I won't be a full-fledged physician till I finish up at Starfleet Medical. Then I'll be signing on a ship someplace. Cadet Kirk . . ."

"Yes, sir?"

"I was just thinking you look familiar. Kirk—I know! Didn't you knock me upside-down during a football game back at the Academy?"

"Was that you?"

"Sure was! You cost me my winter break, buster!"

Unaffected, the cadet tossed off a polite, "Sorry, sir."

But he wasn't sorry. McCoy frowned, but dropped the subject. "What kind of vessel is this?"

"It's a Zodiac-Class Interstellar warp shuttle, sir." Cadet Kirk ground his words out. He obviously wasn't in a mood to talk about the transport after McCoy's insults. His face was still red under the toast-blond wisp of hair that fell over his brow.

McCoy glanced around, back into the main cabin, where Ensign Spock sat reading a manual of some kind. "Looks pretty clunky to me. Hope it holds together."

"It will." The young man twisted in his seat and pointed at the two rows of elbow-shaped supports running along the deck where the side bulkheads met the carpet. "Those beam brackets are the old-style knees, made of heavy-duty cast rhodinium. Above that, you can see the clinker plating, with strakes overlapping like roof shingles. Most of the newer transports are made with flush plating, set edge to edge. The clinker plating is stronger. I wrote a paper on it two months ago. This 'crate,' " he went on, "is exactly that—a crate. No comforts or amenities, and there are only two joiner bulkheads, which are bulkheads that don't contribute to the strength of the hull. No cabin walls and dividers to add weight."

McCoy watched the cadet, who was concentrating very hard on his piloting. On the wide forward screen, the moon rolled by like a big beach ball. There was no real window, but instead a screen that pretended to be a window, showing them what was in front of them. The screen could be switched to show the aft view also, and they would be able to look at whatever they were flying away from.

Soon the cadet gained the nerve to pilot the ship faster and faster at sublight power, and the planets began to wheel by on the curved course that would take them out of the solar system. They were taking a flight path that ran along the plane of the ecliptic, the same imaginary pie plate the planets circled on. They could go "down" or "up" from that circle, but other ships might be using those flight paths.

Earth's sister planets, the others circling this sun, were all in different places, but on this particular flight path the *Spitfire* did pass a couple of them. The huge streaked ball of Jupiter, the gray-blue yarn of Uranus . . . these were among the first planets every Earth child learned.

"How do you know so much about this particular crate?" McCoy asked.

"I slept here last night," Cadet Kirk said.

"Why would you do a thing like that?"

"Because I wanted to get the feel of the craft."

"Couldn't you get the feel of it just by driving it?"

"That's . . . not what I mean."

"All right," the medic allowed, "explain what you mean."

The cadet seemed uneasy at having to clarify his feelings. "Ships have . . . personality."

"Oh. I get it. That thing sailors talk about—how the ship's got some kind of life and pulse and like that. Identity. Aren't all ships of a certain design built exactly alike?"

"No matter how identically the parts are made," Cadet Kirk said, "when they're attached to each other there are always slight differences. That's why every vessel is individually tested and rated for its own tolerance levels. Two ships that seem identical might have different safe top speeds, or different turning-stress levels or braking capabilities."

"But all those are things you learn from actually driving," McCoy pointed out. "What does sleeping in here do for you?"

"It let's the ship know I'm here," the cadet told him slowly. "There's a bond between a ship and her crew. How hard you'll fight for each other . . . how much of a pounding you'll take for each other . . . you get attached. It matters."

McCoy grunted. "Buster," he said, "I wouldn't get that attached to my own liver."

He was getting the idea that this cadet not only flew this bucket, but *liked* the bucket. McCoy thought he'd better be more careful about what comments he made about the *Spitfire.*

"So," he went on, "how long have you been making this run?"

"About twenty minutes, sir."

Sitting bolt upright, McCoy stared at him. "Twenty *minutes?* Are you telling me you've never piloted into deep space before?"

"That's correct, sir. Not alone, anyway."

Grasping the arms of his seat, McCoy sat straight up. "Turn this thing around!"

Chapter
3

"I'm not allowed to turn around," Cadet Kirk said. "Not unless there's an emergency."

"This *is* an emergency!" Leonard McCoy insisted. "I'm putting my life in the hands of another student who's never driven beyond interplanetary spacelanes!"

"Never soloed," the cadet corrected. "I can do it. I earned this, remember?"

"You earned what? Something other than being Richard Daystrom's chauffeur?"

"I also earned the privilege of having a special solo. That usually means going beyond the Agira Basin. This will complete my qualification for my warp rating."

"And I'm your first passenger? Lucky me."

"I'm a certified near-space pilot, Sublight rating. I'm licensed for Earth transports and interplanetary crossings. This voyage'll qualify me for my F.O.S. warp rating."

"F.O.S.?"

"First Open Space."

"How long will it take us to get to Colony Cambria?"

"We should arrive in about three and a half days."

"Three and a half? But I heard the trip would take less than two days!"

"It would if we went straight there. But first I have to drop off a satellite at the Smith-McBride Asteroid Station for a hydrographic survey. Then we have to pass by a Federation automated outpost and pick up its power system numbers."

"How long will that take?"

"No time at all. We're not stopping. We're just swerving by the area and picking up the numbers by remote. Automated stations broadcast them every hour. After

1 9

that we stop at the Tank Barge *Polly Herman* to fuel up. Then I have to inspect a convoy of cattleships—"

"Battleships?"

"Cattleships. Ships that transport livestock to colonies. I have to inspect the pens, the conditions of the animals, the safety and sanitation systems, and make sure everything's up to Starfleet code for live-animal transport."

"We have to be around a herd of cows?"

"Cows, pigs, chickens, sheep, horses, and llamas," the cadet said. "The ships are just called 'cattleships' out of tradition. It actually means any ship rigged for livestock."

"Doesn't sound like very dignified duty for a crisp young preranker like yourself."

"Dignity doesn't matter. Following orders does."

The cadet was still mad. McCoy could tell. And in a way he understood. The young man had struggled to get good grades, earned his chance to make a name for himself as Richard Daystrom's pilot and aide. All that was being left behind at ever-increasing speed.

McCoy watched the grim, ruddy-faced boy. "How old are you, tiger? Nineteen?"

"Going on eighteen. My birthday's next month."

"You're only seventeen?" McCoy blurted.

Cadet Kirk scowled. "You're not much older, sir."

"Older enough." Sitting back, McCoy fell silent and looked at the licensing tag on the *Spitfire*'s bulkhead.

> Cadet James T. Kirk
> Sub-L, N.S.P.
> UFP STARFLEET ACADEMY
> Authorization 405 G

Those must be the ratings Cadet Kirk had just talked about—sublight, near-space pilot . . .

"Ready for warp speed," the cadet said coldly, adjusting the controls before him. Obviously he wasn't the type to waste time. "Warp point five . . . point seven . . . point eight-five," the cadet droned, pressing the full-warp enabler.

Dotted with jewels of distant stars and nebulae, space blew into a wash of streaks. *Crack*—the speed of light!

"Warp one," Cadet Kirk murmured. He stared at the forward screen, as if all this frightened him a little too. But he also seemed proud, and glad to have somebody here to witness this.

Holding his breath, McCoy shifted his eyes from the forward screen to the cadet, then back again. Then to the cadet again. Any minute they'd melt or blow up or something.

Any second . . .

Any time now . . .

"Warp two," Cadet Kirk said.

Warp speed . . . going faster than the speed of light, by actually bending the relationship between time and space. The whole idea sometimes struck him as impossible, and even though space travelers had been using warp speed for a long time, high speeds were always dangerous. Warp speed was dangerous because of the strange, almost magical science involved.

Warping space in order to rush from place to place actually meant putting the ship in another dimension than the planets, stars, and nebulae it was passing. The slightest error could mean cramming into a star or ripping the body of the ship apart.

"Cruising at warp two," Cadet Kirk said, his voice shuddering ever so slightly. He tapped a small panel at his left. "Logging faster than light speed . . . time . . . and stardate."

"Congratulations," McCoy offered.

Cadet Kirk shot him a sideways glare.

"Enjoy yourself," McCoy added quickly. He got up and left the cockpit.

He went back into the main compartment, picked one of the six seats, settled into it, and put his feet up. Maybe if he took a nap, the trip would seem shorter.

Settled in his own lounge, Ensign Spock was deep inside some kind of science manual. The dark-eyed Vulcan offered him only one quick glance, then ignored him.

McCoy thought about snaring the other ensign into a conversation, so he could pick at the Vulcan and tease him a little. That was real fun.

But . . . three and a half days. He'd better save the teasing. He might need it later, to break the boredom. Maybe there were some things to read around here. He leaned and opened a bosun's locker where old magazines and newsletters were sometimes dumped for passengers to leaf through. The locker was full—but with books. Real books, not just computer tapes.

Victory at Aximar by Garth of Izar, Captain, Starfleet. *Celestial Navigation* by Wendy Lesnick. *Computer Guidance in Small Craft* by Orazio Guidal. *Salvage Law* by Michael Riley. The Alexandria Spaceport Foundation's *Seafarers' and Spacefarers' Dictionary. Spacelane Rules of the Road. Maritime Law in the Age of Steam.* Beside it was the same book, only for the Age of Sail.

"Junior," McCoy called. "You studying to be a space lawyer?"

"Me? . . . No, sir. Just want to drive ships."

"What've you got all these dusty books for, then?"

"Some of them are antiques. Two are first editions from the eighteen hundreds."

McCoy shrugged and closed the bosun's locker. He settled deeply into the curved lounge, dimmed the reading light at his side, and closed his eyes. In moments the quiet hum of the *Spitfire*'s warp engines wrapped him like a blanket. He took a deep breath and tried not to think about how fast they were going. He felt himself falling asleep.

As his brain grew foggy, he started thinking about diseases of the human upper respiratory system in alien atmospheres. That was more than enough to carry him to sleep.

His last thought as he drifted off to sleep was about how nice it might be to drowse away a few days without any pressure—

"Zodiac *Spitfire* on Starfleet Emergency Channel ninety-one to Atlantis Outpost! State your intentions!"

McCoy's eyes shot open! Who was that? What was wrong? Why was someone yelling? An alarm of some kind was jangling in the cockpit, and a red light flashed, casting a bloody glow across the salon.

Boom!

A blunt force hit the *Spitfire*, echoing inside its metal bulkheads. The deck tilted to the right, and McCoy went spilling out of his lounge onto the deck carpet.

"What—!" he blurted. Somehow he got to his knees.

A pair of legs dodged past him—Spock. The Vulcan

pulled himself forward against the tilted deck and crawled into the passenger seat in the cockpit.

"What is it, Cadet?" he asked.

For a moment Cadet Kirk pounded at his controls, trying to force the little ship to do what he wanted. But nothing changed—the alert jangle kept ringing, and the ship kept bucking against a force that grabbed it.

"B-Sixty-four Automated Outpost at Atlantis Station! It's throwing a tractor beam on us! We're being pulled off course!"

Chapter
4

"No doubt about it. That's a full-power tractor beam!"

Cadet Kirk spat the words furiously. Before them, the spacescape tumbled drunkenly.

Ensign Spock scoured the readouts. "The engines are buckling," he called out. "I suggest you drop to sublight."

"Sublight, aye," the cadet answered.

As he played the helm, the *Spitfire* suddenly fell out of warp speed and seemed almost to stand still in space. In fact, they were still moving very fast, but not in the right direction, and there was no point going warp speed to the wrong place.

"Atlantis Outpost!" the cadet tried again. "Respond—"

But this time Ensign Spock put his own hand on the communications console and stopped the broadcast. "No signals!"

As the other two stared at him, Spock scowled at the console. "Atlantis Outpost is completely automated. There is no tractor beam there and no one to turn it on if there were one. Someone is doing this deliberately. We should not be contacting them until we know what's happening."

His voice was overlaid by the whooping alarm and the flashing of almost half the lights on the helm control board. Together he and Cadet Kirk battled the force gripping the *Spitfire*.

McCoy watched from between the two seats. "Why would an automated outpost be pulling us off course?" he asked.

"It can't be," Cadet Kirk answered. "Somebody must've installed a tractor device on the station."

Wide-eyed, McCoy shook his head. "But why? I've seen outposts like that. They're just hunks of equipment, usually doing geological surveys and running wells and mines."

The Vulcan palmed the helm. "We're definitely being pulled off course, by a beam from the Atlantis station."

"Can we overcome its pull?" McCoy asked.

Neither Cadet Kirk nor Ensign Spock answered. Clearly they were fighting to do just that. But the whine of the helm and engines said they were failing.

"Can't we pull in the other direction?" McCoy persisted.

"Not if the tractor beam has more power than our ship's thrust," Spock said. "We could burn out our engines in minutes."

"I'd rather fight it," Cadet Kirk said.

The Vulcan twisted to face him. "That makes no sense. I just explained—"

"You'd be right if this ship were over three thousand metric tons. But I think we've got enough thrust to fight the beam."

McCoy looked at him. "You *think?*"

Spock pointed at the sensor grid. "Cadet, the tractor beam is the old magnetic design, originally used for transfer of large cargoes. According to the energy readings, this tractor beam is capable of not only holding this vessel, but breaking it in two."

"There's got to be a way to fight it," the cadet insisted.

To keep from bumping his head again, McCoy lowered himself to one knee. "Is there a problem with your hearing?"

Cadet Kirk frowned at the console before him. "Sir, we've got to contact whoever's doing this and get them to break that beam."

As the cadet reached for the communications panel, Ensign Spock pushed his arm back. "Not yet," the Vulcan told him.

Now the boy's flashing hazel eyes came up sharply. "Are you saying we should go down silent? We don't know if there's anybody controlling the beam. We could be dragged into the planet's surface at full speed—"

"I know that. We have to take the risk."

"Sir, there are certain steps we're supposed to take with any deviation in our flight plan. There are no exceptions. This is my warp solo and I have to do it right!"

"No contact." The Vulcan's answer was crisp and blunt.

Cadet Kirk started to sweat. "Sir, there are rules for this situation. There are rules for *every* situation."

Spock's lively eyes flickered like electricity. "That would be quite illogical, cadet. We should hold off any contact until we find out who is doing this to us, and why."

Leaning between them, McCoy asked, "You smell a trap?"

Spock glanced at him as he powered down the impulse engines to avoid overload. "None of us is of any particular value. Logically, there has to be a better reason for pulling us off course."

"What reason?" Cadet Kirk asked.

"Remember," Spock said, "the *Spitfire* was supposed to have another passenger on board."

The cadet stared at him. "Dr. Daystrom!"

"If the persons controlling the beam think they are getting Daystrom, we should let them believe that as long as possible."

"But, sir," Cadet Kirk argued, "that isn't the correct procedure for an emergency. If this is a malfunction of the station, then Dr. Daystrom's transport could be in the same kind of danger when it comes past here later. We should find out who these people are, so we know what to do."

Keeping very calm, but obviously surprised by the strange turn of events, Spock fought to think around what was happening to them. "We should attempt a safe landing on the outpost, find out what is occurring, secure the area, then take appropriate action."

"But that isn't the right order of procedure."

The Vulcan raised a brow. "I outrank you."

"But the *Spitfire* is signed out to me," the cadet countered. "I'm the only one authorized to pilot her, sir."

"Signing out a vehicle does not countermand seniority of rank."

"But it makes me in charge of the vehicle."

"But not what *happens* to the vehicle outside of your flight plan," Spock pointed out calmly. "This is the most logical course of action. We will make no contact yet."

Cadet Kirk glared and scowled and burned, but there was no changing the Vulcan's mind. A choice had been made by the ranking officer, and that was the course they would follow.

"Sir," he said then, "I suggest we attempt a mayday, at least. We should send out some kind of warning about this, in case Dr. Daystrom's shuttle comes by and gets caught too."

"A distress call?" Spock paused, weighing the ups and downs of that.

McCoy watched as Spock decided what to do. Then the Vulcan said, "Proceed."

The cadet concentrated on deploying a distress call. McCoy watched as he tapped in time, location, identity . . . and pushed the MAYDAY automatic broadcast.

"It's not getting out!" the cadet gasped. "Something's blocking the broadcast!"

Ensign Spock frowned over the readouts. "The tractor beam is scrambling the signal. It must have a very high electromagnetic charge. Cancel the mayday before we have a burnout."

Frustrated, Cadet Kirk clicked off his broadcast. The warp shuttle bucked and tipped this way and that, forcing McCoy to hold on tightly to the cockpit seats. He didn't want to get thrown sideways into a bulkhead and end up with a skull injury.

Before them on the screen now, they saw the small green-and-brown planet where Atlantic Outpost had been raised a few years ago. The planet appeared to be wagging back and forth, turning and wobbling like a ball in a bathtub, but in fact the *Spitfire* was doing the wagging and wobbling.

"The hull's taking strain," Cadet Kirk read off as he watched the numbers on the helm. "We're losing thrust too."

"Cut thrust to minimum," Spock said. "Let them pull us in."

"I'd rather not do that, sir."

"We already had this discussion, cadet."

"I know, but it doesn't make sense to let kidnappers have their way on everything."

"On what, specifically?"

"I don't think we ought to let them pull us to wherever they want us. I mean, why should we let them say what happens at every step?"

McCoy squeezed between them again. "You have some better idea?"

"Yes. I think we should crash-land."

Chapter
5

Both McCoy and Spock simply stared at the younger cadet, as if his head were falling off. Crash-land? On purpose?

"I cannot condone that," Spock said. "Too much risk."

The cadet's bright eyes took on a naughty glint. "Risk can work in our favor."

Spock shook his head. "Such action would be reckless."

"Or it might save our lives," the cadet said. He looked at the forward screen, and there the planet was very close. In fact, all they could see now was a great brown-and-gray landmass flanked by two large bodies of greenish water.

But the cadet was sure he was right. "If we let them pull us in, then they call all the shots. Whatever their plan is, we've got to make it go wrong at every turn."

"How can we judge their intentions?" the Vulcan argued. "They may have a valid excuse for this."

"Not valid enough for me," the younger man shot back. "Starfleet expects me to get the *Spitfire* to Colony Cambria safely. And it expects me to bring you in safe too. Anybody who throws a tractor beam on a vessel without saying why is just a criminal."

"This may be malfunction," Spock insisted. "An error of some kind. Or someone on the planet may need help."

The cadet's brows shot together. "I don't believe that, sir. I don't think you do either. I know one thing—whoever wants to get their hands on us, I don't want to deal on their terms. I want them to have to deal on ours."

"Cadet," Spock said steadily, "this mission has gone off course. When that happens, the senior officer takes over the decision-making process. It's my option to decide what action to take. We will allow ourselves to make a safe landing at the source of the tractor beam. Then we will take one step at a time."

Without moving, McCoy watched them both. Which of these strong personalities would win the moment? One consumed with rules and regulations, the other consumed with logic. *If only I could take notes! What a great experiment this would make!*

If only they weren't about to skid onto the surface of a strange planet—

"Are they bringing us in on a landing trajectory or a burn-up trajectory?" Cadet Kirk suddenly asked. "That'll tell us whether they're trying to kill us or not."

In the copilot's seat, Spock touched the controls and

brought up those numbers. "Angle of approach . . . is a landing angle. Apparently they want us alive."

"They want hostages," the cadet corrected. "Buckle up," he added, feeling for his safety harness and locking it around his hips and chest.

In the copilot's seat, Spock distractedly found his own harness and snapped it on.

McCoy knew he should go into the main compartment and lock himself into a lounge, but if he let go of the seats now he would lose his balance and go crashing. And he was hypnotized by the high-speed rush toward the atmosphere. He couldn't pull himself away.

"We're coming into the atmosphere!" he blurted suddenly. He pointed at the screen, where a white-green haze blurred the shapes of landmasses below.

Wind and dust particles blew past the small craft, and the *Spitfire* began to whistle as if it were being spun at the end of a string. The screen flashed with gusts of atmosphere and clouds.

The craft rocked and shuddered, but held together. Cadet Kirk leaned forward, bit his lip, and concentrated hard. When the ship tilted too far to one side, he brought it back, until it tipped too far the other way. Then he had to compensate again.

Spock was doing something too, but McCoy didn't know what. Braking thrusters, maybe? The two weren't saying anything, but they were cooperating somehow, keeping the shuttle under some control in spite of the powerful tractor beam.

"We're heading straight for the meteorological station on the southern continent," Cadet Kirk said. "The kidnappers must be using it for a headquarters."

"I suggest that we do not yet know," Spock responded, "whether these are kidnappers or not."

"What else can they be?" McCoy asked.

"They could be stranded here, possibly from another crashed vessel. Perhaps they have a tractor beam on their wreck and it's their only way of gaining attention from passing craft."

McCoy glanced at Cadet Kirk, who shifted his eyes but didn't move his head or change his attention.

"That's pretty far-fetched," McCoy said then.

"In space, doctor," the Vulcan told him, "the far-fetched happens every day."

McCoy paused for a moment. That was the first time he'd been called "doctor." How strange and new it sounded, coming from Spock's elegant, precise voice.

Suddenly the shuttle started shaking violently. Was the hull holding together? Were those overlapping seams Cadet Kirk had pointed out to him now coming apart?

The land in front of them changed from a blurry mass to a pattern of hills with trees, and with thin dirt roads cut through them in some places.

"Leveling off," Cadet Kirk strained. He had to squint through a heavy fog in the region. Before them on the screen, thick white haze was interrupted only by lumpy growth popping up under them. "Visibility is seventeen meters—not much at this speed."

"Let the computer guidance take over." Spock touched his controls. "Atlantis Outpost's landing signals will bring us to the pad. Hold the ship as steady as possible. Watch for obstacles . . . sensors are reading some tall trees."

Curious—the Vulcan was willing to take over the decisions about the mission, but not the actual piloting of the craft. Cadet Kirk had been assigned this ship and was expected to fly it in all conditions. Maybe there were legal reasons, regulations, or maybe there was some tradition involved. He didn't know.

A quick jolt to the right broke his grip on the back of Cadet Kirk's seat, and McCoy went sprawling into the tight space behind Spock's seat. He managed to raise his arm and take the impact on his elbow against one of those beam brackets. The movement sent blinding pain running through his upper body.

When he struggled to his knees again, holding his throbbing arm, the *Spitfire* was soaring through open air over some kind of valley floor. On both sides, jagged hills reached up like teeth in a pair of open jaws.

"We're shallowing!" Cadet Kirk shouted over the howl of the engines and alarms. "Force the nose up!"

McCoy hunkered back on the heaving deck, keeping most of his body behind Spock's chair, but peeked out at the main screen. The valley floor shot by, and on the horizon was a complex of flat-topped buildings painted a light green soup color. There were stacked towers of metal attached to the buildings, and several huge portable glass structures like greenhouses scattered on the meteorology station's campus.

That was the place they were being drawn into—Atlantis Outpost.

"There they are," Cadet Kirk said.

McCoy looked up. On the screen, inside the bright

red, yellow, and white circles of the landing pad, were several men watching them come in.

"What're they holding?" he asked.

"Laser rifles, that's what!" Abruptly Cadet Kirk leaned into his controls, snapped off a couple of connections, and took the throttle in his right hand and the steering wheel console in his left. He leaned forward, and the engines whined in response.

"Cadet!" Spock shouted. "We'll overshoot the complex!"

The cadet nodded sharply. "I'll be sure to do that, sir!"

At that instant, the Atlantis complex sheared past beneath them. Instead of veering toward it, the craft muscled past, screaming and fighting against the tractor beam.

"That was not an order!" Spock reached out for the piloting controls. "Stop immediately!"

The cadet put out his own hand, just long enough to nudge Spock back. Not exactly a hit, but a firm bump. "Too late, sir!"

"Release your controls, Cadet!"

"It's too late! Everybody hang on! We're crashing!"

Chapter
6

Blustering noise pounded in Leonard McCoy's throbbing ears. The cabin flashed with violent patches of light and darkness. Hard forces pounded the outer skin of the *Spitfire*—they must be clipping the tops of trees!

Branches reached up and swatted the shuttle as it rollicked closer to the ground. Red and yellow flashers on the console cast terrible shapes on the bulkheads. Those were warning lights—the engines were fighting to keep the ship up, but the tractor beam had dragged it down. Now they had to go all the way down before they could repair things and go back up.

Taking a hammering, the little craft zagged between the trees. McCoy caught sight of Cadet Kirk's muscular arms working back and forth and his shoulders hunching. Then everything went dark.

McCoy felt as if he were sitting inside a kettle drum.

Boom, boom, boom, boom. He hunched his own shoulders, pressed his right side against the back of Spock's seat, and crammed his eyes shut.

Scraaaaaaaatch—

That came from underneath! They were scuffing the ground!

Swerving like a hornet, the *Spitfire* carved a path for itself through the undergrowth, busting branches and smashing the edges of rocks. If one of those rocks struck them just right, it could cut the shuttle open like a melon.

Boom—boom boom boom—Charrrrack—

McCoy's shoulder slammed hard against the seat, his hip driving into the deck. Then he was picked up for a few seconds, and dropped again in a different position, with the side of his face on the carpet. With a final bump, the *Spitfire* skidded to a stop against a solid object out there.

Leaning at a sickening angle, the little ship bleeped and wheezed and gasped. The alarms stopped ringing. The sensors stopped trying to tell them that they were too close to the planet's surface. It was dark in here now.

Were the others alive? There wasn't any sound from either of the pilot seats.

"Ouch."

A voice! Certainly, it wasn't Spock. A Vulcan wouldn't say "ouch." A Vulcan would say, "Noting pain in an extremity."

Must be Cadet Kirk . . .

Invigorated by the sound of a patient in need of help, McCoy found the strength to push himself up. He could see something now—a faint emergency light had popped on. The little light was pink, easier on the eyes than white or yellow. It cast a candy-apple glow on the tilted deck and seats.

At his side, the bulkhead was bent inward as if punched from outside. Of course, that was exactly what had happened. As he gazed at the bulging bulkhead, he noticed that Cadet Kirk had been right—that overlapped clinker plating had held.

McCoy pulled himself up and looked between the seats.

Cadet Kirk sat blinking forward at the dark screen, coughing on puffs of electrical smoke from his console.

McCoy shimmied between the seats. "Are you hurt?"

"I don't think so," the cadet rasped, then coughed again. He reached to his left, punched a toggle, and a ventilator started whirring in the ceiling.

The smoke twisted happily, and raced toward the ventilator.

"Ensign?" McCoy put his hand on the Vulcan's arm. "Spock?"

Spock jolted as if startled, blinked, and looked at him. "We're down," he uttered.

"Yes, we seem to be." Carefully McCoy touched a wound on the upper left side of Spock's face. Green blood dribbled from the abrasion, which was surrounded by a quickly spreading bruise.

"Where are we?" Spock asked, fighting for consciousness.

Cadet Kirk waved at the electrical smoke. "Looks like . . . we came down about fourteen kilometers past the complex."

The Vulcan grasped the console before him and tried

to pull forward. "We have to get out in case the coolant ruptures—"

"Hold still," McCoy told him. "Does this crate have a first-aid kit?"

"Starboard side, aft," Cadet Kirk said as he unbuckled his harness. "I used it for a pillow last night."

"Both of you sit still."

McCoy hurried back along the tilted deck, to the rear part of the ship, then fished around on the starboard side. He found the first-aid kit, a leatherlike pouch with a magnetic pressure seal. Cradling it in one arm, he pulled himself forward again.

By the time he got back, the cadet and the ensign were arguing again.

"As soon as I saw their weapons, I reacted. There wasn't time to ask what I should do. I just did it."

"From now on, Cadet," Spock said instantly, "you will take no action without consulting me. If there's no time, my last orders will stand. Is that clear?"

"Yes, sir, it's clear."

"What is this place?" McCoy asked. "What does Atlantic Outpost actually do?"

"It's a weather-control experimentation station," Cadet Kirk said. "It's part of terraforming this planet for agricultural colonization. But mostly they're trying to figure out just how much weather can be controlled."

"How do they do that?"

"With satellites," Spock filled in. "Computers map out natural weather conditions and project likely changes. Then, satellites are used to redirect the sun's heat to various areas or deprive other areas of warmth."

"Why would anybody want to control weather?"

"Controlling rainfall alone can have a great effect on farming conditions. Barren continents could be made green. Wet areas could be made more arid, better for certain crops and animals. However . . ." Spock winced as McCoy dabbed at his head wound. "Creating weather is one thing . . . manipulating it is another."

"Doesn't sound like such a big deal," McCoy grumbled.

"Oh the contrary," the Vulcan said. "One hurricane has more energy than all the nuclear weapons produced in the entire twentieth century. If that power could be harnessed, it would be a fabulous resource."

"If they can do that on an unpopulated planet like this one," Cadet Kirk filled in, "they'll be able to use it on other planets too. They can put water in places where people are dying of drought, or dry up places where there's too much flooding."

"Sounds good to me," McCoy commented. At the moment he found it hard to care about a little weather control.

"What about a mayday?" the cadet asked then. "We should broadcast one right now, while we have the chance."

"That may not be the wise course," Spock told him.

Cadet Kirk made a motion at the console with one hand. "The beam is off us now. According to regulations, we *have* to broadcast a mayday right away."

"A distress call signal could also be a homing signal." Spock was unbuckling his own harness now. "There is nothing in the regulations dealing with being kidnapped, Cadet."

"But there are regulations that deal with accidents and with crimes. This is one of those. Maybe both."

"Which manuals have you been reading?" McCoy asked as he pressed a patch of sterile gauze to Spock's injury.

"All of them," Cadet Kirk answered. He looked at Spock again. "Sir, now that we're on the ground, we're compelled to follow procedure. We're required to report in, so a search party can be deployed. Otherwise, nobody'll know where or when we were pulled off course. They could search for years and not find us. I'm sending a message with coordinates."

"The kidnappers could zero in on our signal," Spock said. "Then they will be the ones to find us."

"We've got to leave some kind of trail, or we could be stranded on this station for years. I don't think you want that any more than I do." When neither of them dared argue that particular point, the cadet added, "I'm going to send an automated mayday before we lose our power. Then it'll be too late."

McCoy and Spock looked at him, but neither said anything.

"Very well," Spock finally said, "but you send it under my official protest."

"Noted," the cadet said. He reached forward, and deliberately punched in a mayday code with their location, then hit the BROADCAST button.

The cadet looked at Spock for one more second, then pushed out of his seat. He crawled over McCoy, and leaned to check something on the port side of the cockpit.

"We've still got our coolant," he said. "No ruptures

so far. We might be able to take off again if we can get the ship into a clearing. I've got a come-along and four antigravs in back. And there's a laser torch we can use to cut trees."

"Let me up, please," Spock said to McCoy.

"I'll let you up in just a minute," McCoy said. "I want to make sure you don't have a concussion first. A head injury is nothing to play with."

"Hurry," Spock instructed. "We're now working against time."

"Another half meter!"

"Almost there—" McCoy gasped. Together he and Spock heaved on the cable of the hand-held come-along, a contraption made to loop around a tree or rod, then crank its cable tighter and tighter.

Thirty feet away, Cadet Kirk managed two antigravs attached to the *Spitfire*'s bow. The little ship was crammed in between two very big trees. If it had hit either of those trees head-on, it might have disintegrated. But it was just wedged, and with some power and leverage, they could get it out.

Crank, crank, crank—inch after inch, the cable tightened. The shuttle's blocky hull scratched backward toward them. On top of the rectangular-shaped hull, a small communications unit blinked silently, sending their distress beacon into space. Was it strong enough to reach the spacelanes?

Suddenly the shuttle slid harshly to one side, and clunked to the ground.

"That's it!" the cadet called from the bow. "We're clear of the trees." He came jogging toward them. "We should be able to cut our way out of these bushes, then antigrav the *Spitfire* over to that clearing."

"What good will it do to get to the clearing?" McCoy asked. "We can't take off, just to get caught in that tractor beam again."

"We might be able to skim the planet's surface and find another angle away from here."

Spock straightened and rubbed his hands, which were grooved and sore from gripping the come-along's handle. "That's assuming the tractor beam has a narrow band. If it has wide one, we may end up crashing again. We may not be so fortunate a second time."

"Then we have to turn off the tractor beam at the source."

McCoy looked at him, then at Spock, and waited for an argument to break out. He was licking his chops about which side to take when Spock surprised him completely by saying, "That . . . is very logical."

The cadet shifted his feet and his face flushed a little. He appeared almost embarrassed by getting the Vulcan's approval, which seemed to be rare indeed. "Then that's the plan?"

"I would accept that as a primary goal," Spock said coldly. "We shall see if it proves more dangerous than it sounds."

The Vulcan walked away, to the other side of the shuttle.

So much for approval.

Deprived of his victory, Cadet Kirk clamped his mouth shut and dodged inside. He came out again with two laser torches. Tossing one to McCoy, he grimly set about cutting away the branches and vines that had snared the *Spitfire*.

"I guess I should help," McCoy muttered, and tried to figure out which end of the torch the laser beam came out of.

Just when he found the business end, a loud whine cut through the air around them as if out of nowhere. He looked around, into the sky where the sound was coming from.

Cadet Kirk came dodging out of the bushes, craning at the sky. Ensign Spock reappeared from behind the shuttle.

Before anyone could speak, two small buzzardlike craft soared in at them and strafed the crash site.

"They found us!" Cadet Kirk blurted.

"They followed our mayday beacon," Spock called over the howl of the circling attack crafts.

There were two of them, small two-man atmospheric vehicles, very common, used for everything from regional defense to taxicab service. They weren't Starfleet craft, but just common, everyday planetary runabouts.

They swooped down to have a look at the three castaways, then veered off and came around for another pass. As they came around, a narrow white glow appeared on the nose of each craft.

"Take cover!" Cadet Kirk called. He waved them toward the trees. "They just armed their weapons!"

Chapter
7

Heavy laser bolts slashed through the bushes, burning the leaves and raising a terrible stink. Insects clouded upward. Sizzling branches crackled through the shaken trees and hit the ground inches from McCoy's huddling body.

He had run, but he had stumbled. Spock and Cadet Kirk were somewhere in the bushes too, but he couldn't see them. His heart pounded in his chest. Why would these people kidnap them, then try to fry them with lasers?

Without raising his head more than a few inches, he shimmied under the bushes, through the dry moss and decaying vegetation.

Teeeeшшшш тееешшш тешш—lasers again!

McCoy kept his head down. Bark and stones sprayed across his spine.

"This way!"

He looked up in the direction of the cadet's voice, then crawled toward the sound.

As the lasers pounded the earth again only ten feet away, two sets of hands grasped him and pulled him under cover of a fallen log. He found himself curled between the cadet and Ensign Spock.

"How did they find us so fast?" he asked.

Spock squinted at their attackers. "The mayday signal. I was concerned about exactly this."

Cadet Kirk glanced at him, frustrated that following regulations had gotten them into deeper trouble.

"Why are they shooting at us?" McCoy wondered. "If they want hostages, why are they trying to kill us?"

"They're not," the cadet said bluntly.

Digging an elbow into the moss, McCoy craned to look at him. "What do you mean, they're not!"

"The laser bolts are hitting ten feet in that direction, and ten feet in the other direction. They're firing at a column around us. They're trying to scare us, not kill us."

"Then they *do* want hostages," Spock concluded.

The cadet peered out at the two small craft, which were now circling for a landing. "They want Richard Daystrom."

"Then we should contact them," the Vulcan said. "Tell them who we are. Once they discover that Dr. Daystrom is not among us, logically they will not pursue the actions they're taking. They won't want to risk a kidnapping charge for no profit. When they land, we'll identify ourselves."

The two craft were already on the ground, still buzzing

with power and glowing with their power-packed weapons.

"Permission to speak, sir," Cadet Kirk said then. He looked as if a light had gone on in his head.

"Yes?" Spock responded.

"Well . . . what if they *don't* think that? Or what if they don't care about kidnapping charges? What if they don't even care about a murder charge?"

"That's true," McCoy agreed. "Just because we present them with logic doesn't mean they'll react like Vulcans."

"What is the alternative?" Spock peered at them both, unable to think of any other way than simple, direct logic.

Cadet Kirk suggested, "We have to fight our way out."

McCoy looked around. "Fight our way to where? Our shuttle is here. You mean get inside it and fight?"

"It'll take time to clear the branches away," Spock said. "We have no time."

Cadet Kirk looked out at the highlands to the west. "We can get away from them, then make our way into those hills and hide out until a rescue detail shows up. The distress call went out," he added, pinning Spock with a glance, "and all we have to do is hold our own until they come."

"They might be coming into a trap because of us," Spock pointed out.

"That's their job, sir," the cadet said unapologetically. "It'll be mine someday. Our job right now is to be alive and well when they get here. We can do that if we can get to those hills."

"We have to try negotiating first," Spock said.

Cadet Kirk ducked under a branch to look at him. "I respectfully remind you, sir, that regulations specifically say that no Starfleet personnel should negotiate with terrorists."

"There's a time and place for everything," McCoy said warily watching the nearby craft. "We're unarmed, aren't we?"

"We might be able to fake something," Cadet Kirk said. "I'll see what's aboard."

He dodged back behind the log as six kidnappers appeared outside their small crafts.

"Humans," McCoy said automatically. "Ooops—there's one Klingon among them! Look at that! I've only seen two Klingons in my whole life, and there's another one!"

"I've never seen any at all!" Cadet Kirk mentioned, peering through the leaves at the dangerous-looking men coming toward them, carrying hand-held weapons. "They don't move freely in Federation space, do they?"

"No," Spock said sharply.

The cadet smirked briefly, then scooted away behind them into the trees and bushes.

"Usually they keep to themselves," McCoy added. "Unless they want to cause trouble, that is." He turned to Spock. "You and I are scientists. I'd feel better if I were trying to argue a point with a dish of bacteria. He's not a scientist." He nodded in the direction Cadet Kirk had gone. "Maybe he's got a better instinct about this kind of thing. Certainly better than you, right? After all, Vulcans and instinct don't get along, do you?"

Clearly irritated, Spock squinted through the bushes. "Not lately."

"What do you want to do?"

"The cadet is well-intentioned, but hotheaded. I prefer to contact these men. Find out their terms."

The six men moved in their general direction, aiming their laser rifles, clearly looking for target. They seemed ready to shoot, and a shiver went down McCoy's spine as he anticipated the graze of hot energy crossing his body. One of those lasers could cut a person right in half, or slice off a leg and seal the wound in one swipe.

"I'll speak to them," Spock said. "You stay down."

"No argument here," McCoy muttered.

Spock arranged his feet under him, preparing to stand up and face the men—

Zzzzztt—Craaacccck

McCoy ducked, and so did Spock. What had happened? Had the men shot at them? Had the lasers cut into the trees overhead?

Cadet Kirk crouched halfway up the trunk of the tree, holding on with one hand, and holding a laser torch in the other hand. He was cutting a branch. With a silly little laser torch!

Suddenly the huge branch shuddered, snapped at the base, thundered through the other branches, and came down on the heads of two of the kidnappers, driving them to the ground!

Chapter
8

"Cadet! Belay that action!"

Spock raised his voice enough for the cadet to hear, and McCoy was pretty sure the approaching kidnappers clearly heard him too. They would know, now, that the attack was broken off on purpose. Maybe that would even work in Spock's favor if he intended to try talking to these rough-looking people.

The cadet lowered his laser torch and looked at Spock from the protection of the tree's trunk.

Spock motioned him to stay where he was, but the cadet was already halfway back to them. The young man skittered through the bushes and crouched near McCoy.

"Sir?" he asked the Vulcan. "I thought we were going to defend ourselves."

"I have decided to attempt negotiation," Spock said.

"You mean we're giving up? Just like that?"

"I have no intention of surrendering, Cadet. In fact, I will not order the two of you to associate with these people. But as a Vulcan I have an obligation to attempt to negotiate, to find a common ground. They will be forced to make a new plan when they discover Dr. Daystrom is not here. We may be able to come to some compromise."

Cadet Kirk didn't like what he was hearing. His mouth worked with things he was about to say, but which he held back. Finally he pressed his lips tight and kept quiet.

"Just in case they aren't impressed with Vulcan philosophy," McCoy asked, "what do we do then?"

"Escape," the Vulcan said without inflection. "Follow the cadet's original plan. Hide in the hills. Wait for rescue."

Spock raised both hands high and turned toward the kidnappers. He counted off a few seconds during which just his raised hands showed over the bushes, then very slowly, making sure they could see him clearly, he stood up.

"Come on out here. All the way out. Hands up," one of the kidnappers called.

"You Starfleet?" another asked.

The Klingon swatted his comrade across the chest. "Of course Starfleet, you idiot! What else is that uniform?"

Cadet Kirk hunched toward McCoy. Together they watched as Spock made his way through the bushes to the open ground, then walked evenly toward the kidnappers.

"You think he knows what he's doing?" the cadet asked.

"I think *he* thinks so. He's got a couple thousand years of Vulcan philosophy backing him up—"

"What if those men haven't read Vulcan philosophy? Compromise usually means that somebody loses, and it's not usually the guys with the guns."

They watched for a few moments while Spock was questioned by two of the men and the Klingon, while the other man stood back and waited. The other two, whom Cadet Kirk had dropped the branch onto, were struggling to their feet and trying to collect their senses.

McCoy tried to evaluate what he was seeing. Was the Klingon in charge out there? Or the big red-haired man with the moustache? Perhaps it was the small-boned bald man with the space between his teeth. They were all talking to Spock, one by one. The only men not talking to him were the two who'd been injured, and the one other, a tall, skinny fellow with black hair cut very short and sticking straight up from his head like a currying brush.

"Ensign Spock's not telling them much," Cadet Kirk said suddenly. "He's trying to get information out of them without giving them any."

"How can you tell?"

"Because they're still asking questions. If they'd found out what they wanted to know, they wouldn't be asking so much. Every time one of them asks something, Spock gives a long answer. He's making stuff up."

Trying to pay attention, McCoy watched the way the men were speaking to Spock, and decided that the cadet might be right. Spock was doing a lot of talking, but McCoy guessed he wasn't saying very much of any value.

"That's the leader, over there," the cadet said suddenly.

"Which? The Klingon?"

"No. The black-haired one."

"The one over to the side? But he's not saying anything. He's just watching."

"I know," the cadet confirmed. "He's watching, and the others are glancing at him every time they ask a question. Listen—if we have to run for the hills, I want you to go first."

Over their shoulders, McCoy could see the hills, but had doubts about running to them without being cut down by those laser rifles.

"If I go first," he asked, "what will you be doing?"

"This laser torch doesn't have much range, but it's enough to set fire to these bushes. I'll make a firewall to cover our escape. I don't want to have to worry about you while I do it."

"Oh, you won't have to worry about this country boy, believe me. I've got long, long legs. They get longer when there's a rifle pointed at my back."

"Don't blame you." The cadet paused. "You know what? I don't even know your name."

"Oh . . . it's Leonard. Hi."

"Hi." The cadet chuckled. "I'm Jimmy. James T. Kirk."

"I know. I read the I.D. on the—"

"Look! The black-haired one's moving in!"

"Shh!" McCoy motioned him silent as they watched.

Looked like the cadet was right. As the thin man with the short black hair came closer, the others moved back. Even the Klingon.

That sight alone—a Klingon backing off from a human—was scary. What kind of man was this?

The skinny man fixed his eyes on Ensign Spock. He was a little taller than Spock and was able to tuck his chin just a bit as he moved closer. He stared without blinking, like a cat stalking a bird.

And Spock was certainly like a bird, like a raven—a smart, dark raven. He stood there elegantly, a slim pillar of Starfleet control. The bright sunlight flickered on his ink-black hair.

Suddenly the skinny man lashed out with the butt of his laser rifle and cracked Spock across the side of his head. Spock managed to tip his head away at the last second, easing the blow somewhat, but it was still a hard knock. Spock went sprawling on the crisp dirt and rocks.

"That's it," Cadet Kirk said. "Spock just told them that Dr. Daystrom isn't with us. Now the head guy is mad."

The skinny man shouted a single order—McCoy didn't pick up the word as it echoed against the back hills— and the Klingon and the red-haired man moved in on Spock. They dragged him to his feet and shackled his arms behind him.

Then, with the butt of a laser rifle crammed into his back, they shoved him away, toward one of their little craft.

"They're taking him prisoner!" McCoy gasped.

"Come on!" Cadet Kirk grabbed his arm and pulled. "Let's get out of here!"

Chapter
9

"Keep running!"

"I am!"

McCoy already felt as if he'd run two miles. His lungs heaved and his heart hammered in his chest. His thighs ached and his mind sang with the sound of laser rifles whining behind him.

"This way!"

Cadet Kirk's voice buzzed in his ear. He tilted toward it and kept running. Rocks rose under his feet, then cliffs rose around him, and he dodged for cover in the higher ground.

Behind them, the stand of dry bushes burned furiously, providing them with cover as they dodged through the trees.

"What about the shuttle?" McCoy called to the cadet as they climbed higher into the protective rocky hills.

"It has a fire prevention system. When the outer skin reaches a certain temperature, fire retardant will be sprayed all over the craft. It'll be just fine, and waiting for us when we get back."

"We're going back?"

"Eventually. I'm not going to abandon my first command."

"Your first 'command' . . . aren't you getting a little full of yourself? You haven't even been in Starfleet Academy for a whole year yet!"

"Doesn't matter." The cadet veered off to his left and disappeared behind a jutting boulder. "Here's a place to hide."

Panting, McCoy struggled to get up there, and found the cadet huddled in a natural fortress of rock and scrubby bushes. The ground beneath them was almost level. They could defend this place pretty well just by throwing stones, if they had to.

"You think they'll come after us?" McCoy asked.

Cadet Kirk wiped his brow with a sleeve. "No way to know. Probably."

"Probably," the medic echoed sourly. "In a couple of hours, it'll be dark. We'll have to make some kind of plan. We can't stay here in these rocks very long without food or water. So, Mr. Cadet, future commander, go ahead and give an order . . . what do we do now?"

"Keep your head down."

"My head *is* down."

"And don't talk."

"Who's talking? You're the one who's talking!"

"Shh!"

Darkness had fallen swiftly, like an ax blade coming down. Half an hour later, this planet's three bright moons had come drowsily up from behind the horizon, casting sharp, black shadows from the trees and rocks.

Crawling behind Jimmy Kirk's compact body, Leonard McCoy wondered how he'd ended up here when all this started out as a perfectly simple, ordinary ride to a seminar. Now he was scooting on his belly through bushes and over stones, trying to reach the two parked runabouts, six desperate criminals, and one captured Vulcan.

From here, under the light of the three moons, two of them full moons and one a pinkish crescent, he could see the smoldering remains of the stand of trees where the *Spitfire* had crashed. In fact, he could even see the shuttle, its hull crusted white with fire retardant it had sprayed all over itself when the flames touched it. Now it was a dirty mess, but it wasn't burned.

"I only see three of them."

"The other three must be off looking for us," Jimmy said. "I'd guess that, anyway. They're not around here, that's for sure. Why else would those three stick around?"

"Do you know what you're doing?"

"Don't worry. This is a textbook rescue attempt."

"What if these men never read the textbook?"

"First," Jimmy whispered, ignoring McCoy's warning, "we have to get our hands on one of those laser rifles. Once we're armed, they'll have to take us seriously. Then we can rescue Ensign Spock, disable those two runabouts, haul the *Spitfire* out of the bushes, and get out of here and warn Starfleet about these creeps."

"We're going to do all that, are we? I'm getting tired just thinking about it."

"I'll get the weapon . . . you free Ensign Spock. All right, let's move in."

Well, the cadet was decisive, for sure. Whether the decisions were right or not—that remained to be seen. So far, the track record wasn't too good.

But he was still trying. He wasn't giving up. The more he failed, the more determined he got.

McCoy's mind started to wander as he watched Jimmy Kirk sneak along in front of him. Maybe this would make a good research paper. The psychology of refusing to give up. He knew there were people like that in history, like General Ulyssess S. Grant, who treated every defeat like a victory and kept on surging forward until the American Civil War was won for the Union. No matter what disasters befell him, he kept on coming. They called him "Unconditional Surrender" Grant.

This boy was like that. Would the results be as good?

McCoy had no way to know, and he was afraid to guess.

Abruptly, Cadet Kirk surged forward into the darkness toward one of the two little craft. McCoy strained to see, but could only hear the grunts and punches of a wrestling match. Jimmy had charged one of these men and attacked him!

Taking his cue, McCoy got his feet under him and also moved. He skirted around the nearest craft and headed for the second one, where Spock sat with his hands tied behind his back, and his feet tied at the ankles, leaning against the landing strut. His mouth was gagged with a wide piece of black nonconductive tape.

McCoy could see the other two men standing together several yards away, facing the hills and talking to each other. They hadn't noticed what Jimmy Kirk was doing on the other side of the other runabout.

With his pulse throbbing in his ears, McCoy was aware of every tiny crunch of his toes on the rocky ground. Every scratch sounded like a foghorn to him. He kept glancing at the two men, sure that any second they would swing around and fire their laser rifles at him.

Spock saw him now . . . shook his head sharply as if he wanted them to abandon their attempt . . . but he didn't move . . . didn't attract any attention . . .

Stay still . . . don't make any noise . . . almost there . . .

McCoy reached out. Another inch . . . he touched Spock's knee, felt his way down to the shackles tying Spock's ankles. The Vulcan remained motionless, but tense. McCoy could feel the tightened muscles as he tried to loosen the tied polymer strands.

These strips were simple, cheap, but effective too. The knots were locked tight, and the stuff wouldn't stretch. Jimmy Kirk's laser torch might do the trick, or it might melt the plastic to hot liquid and burn Spock's legs and hands. How could he get it off?

If only he had that first-aid kit. There was a scalpel in there, sharp enough to cut the strips. But it was fifty feet away, inside the encrusted *Spitfire*.

"I can't get you loose," he whispered, barely loud enough even to hear himself. He knew Spock would hear him, because Vulcans' hearing was more sensitive than humans'.

"Mmm!" Spock nodded toward the other runabout, but couldn't speak past the tape.

"Quiet." McCoy got to his own feet and slipped both hands under Spock's arm and pulled.

With the faintest shuffle, Spock scratched to his feet, pressing one shoulder against the runabout for leverage. He never took his eyes off the two guards.

"Is that the Klingon?" McCoy murmured, nodding toward the person on the right, who was large and muscular in the hazy yellow moonslight.

Spock nodded, rather furiously, as if still trying to get a message across. He began taking impossibly small steps . . . a few inches at a time . . . McCoy kept a grip on his arm to keep him from toppling over. If they could get to the other side of the runabout . . .

Then what?

They would have to find something sharp and cut those plastic strands.

Hobbling pathetically, Spock made a valiant effort to shuffle out of the line of fire. McCoy's mind reeled with crazy ideas about how to get the plastic strands off.

Bite them? Teeth were good, but not that good.

Stretch them?—no, that wouldn't work, or the tied-up person could just pull his way out.

He thought again of that laser torch. There might be no other choice. Spock might have to deal with some burns in order to escape.

What could McCoy use to treat burns around here? Was there any plant like the aloe native to his planet? Some natural remedy he could use? He wasn't comfortable with those things, even though his great-grandmother in Georgia had raised him on tales of home remedies. In fact, that was where he'd first gotten the idea of becoming a doctor.

Still, the thought of treating laser burns with leaves and sap didn't make him very happy.

He almost jumped out of his skin as a third form appeared silently beside him—Jimmy Kirk!

"Move," the cadet whispered, and nudged McCoy aside.

A short, stumpy blade flickered in the peaches-and-cream moonslight. A knife! He must've taken it off the man he attacked! And he had the man's laser rifle under the other arm!

McCoy stifled a whoop of victory and slid to one side. Jimmy went to work on Spock's bindings. *Snap!* Spaghettilike polymer fell from Spock's ankles. *Snap!* His hands were free.

The Vulcan raised both hands and ripped the tape from his mouth and shouted, "Run! It's a trap!"

Chapter 10

Cadet Kirk was so shocked that he stood frozen in place for three critical seconds. Ensign Spock had to reach to him, spin him around, and yell, "Go!"

"Swingle!" A shot from the Klingon almost knocked McCoy's head off. "Joe! Come out now!"

Scarcely more than a shadow at his side, Spock gave the medic a sharp push too, and less than a second later the red beam of rifle laser seared into the nose of the runabout right where McCoy's head had just been. He felt the electrical charge snap through the air. The buzz of energy raised the hairs on the back of his neck as he dodged away. He caught his boot on a stone and went sprawling. Sparks rained onto his bare face and hands, making a hundred tiny scorch marks.

A side hatch whined open on the runabout closest to them, and the three men who were supposedly in

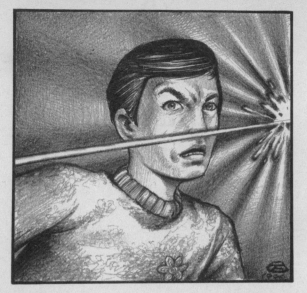

the hills searching for them came rushing out! It *was* a trap!

Spock was trying to haul him to his feet when more laser bolts cut through the open air overhead and drove them both to the ground. When McCoy looked up, they were surrounded. The muzzles of four laser rifles bobbed inches from his head and shoulders. He and Spock were caught.

He tried to see Jimmy Kirk, and wondered why the cadet hadn't used the laser rifle when he had the chance—but then realized that, if this was a trap, these men expected them to come here and wouldn't let them get their hands on a charged rifle.

Sure enough, he saw Jimmy crouch and try to shoot, but the rifle just buzzed flatly, its energy cartridge drained. The red-haired kidnapper tackled Jimmy, drove him to the ground, and yanked away the laser rifle.

Jimmy twisted around on the ground, lashed out with the heel of his boot, and clipped the red-haired man in the chin, knocking him flat.

But it was only one hit, and it was instantly over.

The other men instantly surrounded the cadet.

Above McCoy and Spock, the thin black-haired man glared down in scalding anger. "Get up," he said, his words like acid. Then he looked past them and snapped, "Bring that one over here, Zenoviev. Get him over here!"

"I'm comin', I'm comin'." The burly redhead appeared out of the shadows, shoving Jimmy Kirk roughly in front of him. "He hit me, Joe."

"Aw, he hit you. Poor you." The man called Joe Swingle cocked a hip and mewled without sympathy at the big man. "He hit Crawler too. So what? You need a cotton ball? We'll stick it up your face. Maybe it'll keep both of you quiet."

Hmm, McCoy thought, *sweet guy.*

"Line 'em up," Swingle cracked. He waited until all three young men were shoved arm to arm and held there with well-aimed laser rifles. Then he asked, "Who are you punks?"

"Starfleet to you," Jimmy Kirk snapped back, matching the man's acidic tone.

McCoy felt his eyes go wide and he held his breath. Talk about asking for trouble!

"Oh, goody—a hotshot," Swingle moaned. "That's all I need. You want to be brilliant, smarty? Tell me how come I expend good energy yanking a transport off course and all I get is three piglets in standard sparkle. Where's Richard Daystrom?"

"Not here."

"I can see that, pinky. Who are you anyway? You're not an officer—"

Jimmy stuck his chin out. "Maybe I'm in disguise."

"Yeah. A teddy bear disguised as a plebe. Hey, fellas, look at his baby-face, will ya? How old are you, baby boy?"

"Seventy-two. I'm well preserved. Who are you?"

"I'm a shanghai specialist, little man. I'm a hijacker, and I don't like it when I spend a lot of time and expense setting up a hijacking plan and end up hijacking for no good reason. You cadets are no good reason for sure. So if you want to keep your value as a living creature, you'd better tell me why Richard Daystrom isn't on his assigned transport."

"He didn't want to be exposed to you," Jimmy said. "He's allergic to slime."

Swingle responded to the cadet's insult with a tooth-jarring slam across the face with the back of his hand. Jimmy went sprawling backward into the Klingon, who shoved him to the ground.

Spock flinched, but was pressed back by Zenoviev's laser rifle.

"Easy, ears," the big man rumbled, and flicked one of Spock's pointed ears.

The Vulcan tilted away, but made no other move.

"My commander will not like this," the Klingon snarled. "He paid you to get a computer expert, not a shipload of cadets."

"You keep your mouth shut," Swingle said. "I'll make

good on my part of the deal. Awright," he drawled, "let's get back to the compound. Klaag, you get on the communication web, find out when the next transport comes through here, see if you can dig up a passenger manifest that's accurate this time. Zenoviev, you and Crawler slam these three junior jockeys in a box till I figure out what to do. Maybe we can trade 'em for Daystrom. Starfleet'll have to pay attention when we tell them we've got three of their cherubs on ice. Let's go, before I decide to wipe that smug look off baby boy's face."

The "box" was a janitor's shed on the Atlantis Outpost compound. And it was just about a real box—four steel walls, used as a storeroom for tubs of cleaning fluids, janitorial supplies, brushes, brooms, a tin of rubber gloves, and that was about all.

"We've been kidnapped by this Joe Swingle and his crew, who evidently work for a Klingon commander. The Klingon commander hopes to capture Richard Daystrom for his computer innovations, then hold him for ransom. Swingle wants his cut and seems to be ruthless about getting it. He was furious when he discovered Dr. Daystrom was not among us."

Ensign Spock wasn't happy. He hovered on one spot near the bolted door of the shed, thinking out their problem.

McCoy had watched him for a half hour now, curious about watching a Vulcan stew with anger and battle to hold it in. He was sure he could see the boiling frustrating *just* beneath the surface of that resolute expression.

Spock's face was like a mask, but he was clearly vexed as he glared at Leonard McCoy and Jimmy Kirk.

"Why did you attempt to rescue me?" he asked. "Now you are also captured. What have you gained by your risk? Regulations specify that you were compelled to wait for reinforcements."

Sitting in a corner, Jimmy Kirk grumpily lied, "Maybe I never heard of that regulation."

He hugged his knees and looked away.

McCoy felt sorry for him. The poor cadet had tried to do the right thing step after step, and everything he had done backfired. He was trying to be flexible, to combine rules and regulations with improvisation, but somehow he hadn't learned the recipe yet.

Shifting toward the young man, McCoy quietly said, "It's not your fault, you know."

Jimmy Kirk sulked more deeply, angry with himself and everything around him.

Then he sighed. "I don't get this. . . . I followed regulations, sent out a mayday, and it brought them down on us. I tried to stage a textbook rescue, and they were ready for us every step. They *knew* I'd try what I tried. If regulations give you away to your enemy, what good are they? How can following regulations get us into deeper trouble? I thought Starfleet had all this figured out."

"You're dreaming," McCoy grumbled. "Nobody can guess everything that might happen. Not even Starfleet. First they teach you all the regulations, then later they teach you what to do when regulations don't apply."

The cadet grimaced. "What? What's that supposed to mean?"

Trying to think of a good way to illustrate his point, McCoy pressed his shoulder against the wall. "You ever taken a vacation at the beach?"

"Sure."

"Did your mother ever tell you not to go in swimming alone?"

"Of course."

"And if you saw a two-year-old kid drowning, would you jump in alone anyway?"

"Of course!"

"See? Regulations don't cover everything. That's why we have a command structure—because experience counts for something. When you're little, the rule is 'Do what your mother says.' Later you learn how and when to bend that rule. At the Academy, they start with 'Follow regulations.' Later . . . well, you learn how and when to improvise."

Troubled, Cadet Kirk stared at the rocks, then up at the distant fire, which was already beginning to go out and turn to puffs of black smoke.

"How can I know when?" he asked then.

McCoy offered a shrug. "That's what years of experience are for. I guess you find out if you did the right thing when they either court-martial you or put a medal on you."

Staring at the fire, Cadet Kirk seemed to be truly concerned that he had followed regulations and gotten them into deeper trouble, gotten Spock captured, and now didn't know what to do next. The idea that there wasn't a regulation for everything, or that he might have to fake his way out of this trouble really bothered him.

"Don't let all this get to you," the young medic offered. "Everybody does his best, and after that somebody else takes over. That's the way it is."

"Maybe. But I don't have to like it. They don't take us seriously."

"Who?"

"The bad guys. They lock us up in a shed like dogs because they don't think we can hurt them."

"We can't! We're just Academy students, not full-fledged Starfleet officers."

Jimmy's eyes grew narrow again. He really hated what he was hearing. He didn't like not being taken seriously.

"Look, I've seen a lot like you," McCoy said. "Starfleet's teaching you to follow orders, but eventually they're going to want you to learn when *not* to follow them. When orders don't fit the situation, you've got to bend. That's what a good officer is."

Jimmy Kirk's flashing hazel eyes narrowed. "How do you know?"

McCoy shrugged. "Because that's what a good medic is too."

With that hot sideward glare, Jimmy dissected McCoy, until McCoy felt as if the boy could see right into his head.

Then the cadet looked away again. "Maybe . . . that's how I could've beaten him. . . ."

"Who?" McCoy asked.

Jimmy glanced at him, as if he'd let some secret out. He tightened his grip on his knees. "A senior at the Academy who picks on me all the time."

"Picks on you?"

"Yes."

"What do you do?"

"Nothing. I just stand there and take it."

"Why?"

"Because it's—" Jimmy paused, embarrassed. Then he admitted, "It's against Academy regulations to hit an upperclassman."

"It's against regulations to hit anybody," McCoy said. "This kid actually hits you?"

"All the time."

"Hmm." McCoy stretched his legs out in front of him and looked at his shoes. "It's not allowed to harass an underclassman that way. Why didn't you report him?"

"Because we're supposed to handle things ourselves."

"Well, as I said, when regulations don't fit . . ."

"Are you saying I should've hit him back?"

McCoy shrugged. "Seems to me that he knew you were paralyzed by not knowing what to do. So you did the predictable thing. Maybe if you'd just acted unpredictably one time, he might've thought twice about picking on you."

"I wish I had, now," Jimmy sighed. "Doesn't matter anymore, though. He's been transferred to a ship. I'll probably never see him again."

"Oh, well, sooner or later every bully gets what he deserves."

"I hope so," the cadet agreed. "Only, now . . . I want to be the one to give it to him."

There was a new fire in his eyes, a new muscle to his tone of voice. He really wanted to go out and hit somebody now, to burn off all the anger he felt at having failed again and again.

"How am I going to learn when to break the rules for

the right reasons?" he asked, his voice very quiet. "What do I do first?"

"I don't know," McCoy admitted. "Medics don't have to make that kind of decision. We just patch you cannonballs together after you plow through each other's hulls."

"Your lesson is quaint," Spock interrupted then, turning toward them, "but dangerously illogical, Doctor."

"Oh?" McCoy leaned back, folded his own arms, and looked up at him. "Well, suppose you just polish it up for me, since we seem to suddenly have time on our hands."

The young Vulcan, tall and lean, his head nearly touching the ceiling of the shed, folded his arms casually. "Sending the signal was regulation procedure. This time strict adherence to regulations happened to work against us, as I suspected it might. But we have them for good reason. There are rules about when to send distress signals, when to fight battles, how to pilot ships, how to handle supplies, even regulations on how we should treat each other. Although there are instances where following rules may not be the most efficient thing to do, overall we get the best results when we follow regulations. That is why we have senior officers and the rank system—experience is crucial in balancing the rules with the situation. Experience which, unfortunately, we all lack. You should never take casually the importance of following the rules, Cadet. What you did was right."

"Right?" the cadet asked, disbelieving.

"Yes. You followed textbook strategy for rescue. The area appeared relatively unguarded, the odds close, and although I might disagree with your decision to attempt to rescue me, I do understand the logic of it."

"But they expected us to do that and they set up a trap for us!" Jimmy protested. "I fell right into it."

"Yes, this time logic and predictability worked against you. However, you would hardly have tried to rescue me when I was most heavily guarded, rather than the most lightly guarded."

"I might, now," the boy said roughly. "That might be the time they'd least expect it. Maybe next time I'll try that."

"If there *is* a next time," McCoy tossed in.

Jimmy shook his head. "Maybe I'm not cut out to make command decisions. I'll probably be a cadet all my life."

His face turned ruddy with anger again. He didn't say anything else.

"Well, now that we have something to chalk up to experience," McCoy went on, "what do we do?"

His arms still folded, Spock paced a few steps this way and that, running his thumb along his lower lip. "I have assessed the situation and I determine that the best action is to wait for Starfleet either to pick up our distress broadcast or to log us missing. They will dispatch a security detail to the area and attempt to track the exhaust trail of the *Spitfire*. These mercenaries are armed, dangerous, and they are working for the Klingons, so anything that happens here might be a powder keg. Whatever we do might explode into a diplomatic nightmare for the Federation. Therefore, for us, the wisest action to take is no action. Swingle and his men will consider us harmless and may stop paying attention to us. We will at least be safe."

"Sounds fine to me." McCoy crossed his legs. "I guess I might as well make myself comfortable."

"Wait a minute." Jimmy didn't look up, but scowled at a pile of bottles of chemicals. "All that would be fine if we were fighting Vulcans." Now he looked up and added, "But if I were these guys, I wouldn't think like that. If we don't try to think like them, how can we expect to beat them?"

McCoy fixed a studious glower on the boy. Brother, did this kid learn fast! The medic watched as a key character trait seeded itself in the seventeen-year-old cadet. Jimmy had analyzed in his head Spock's hope of beating these men the decent, logical, predictable way, and was now deciding that decency might not work against indecent people.

Jimmy got to his feet and faced Spock. "I still feel like Dr. Daystrom is my responsibility. If I can keep these criminals from getting their hands on him, I want to do it."

Facing him squarely, Spock lowered his arms to his sides and straightened. "We are unarmed and locked up. Your intentions are noble, but useless. I suggest you sit down and save your energy, in case these men decide not to give us food or water. We'll need all our strength, in case the stay is a long one. By being predictable, we allowed ourselves to be captured. Now, by being predictable again, we may save our own lives."

With a sigh, McCoy pursed his lips, but didn't say anything. Jimmy Kirk didn't say anything either, but he was sizzling with frustration. He hated being cooped up like this. He glared at Spock for a few seconds, then stalked off to the other end of the shed. He disappeared behind a large pile of paint drums.

McCoy stood up and murmured to Spock, "He doesn't like this. Can't say I blame him."

"I would prefer an alternative, if there were one," the Vulcan admitted. "However, this is the logical course to save our own lives. We should remain calm, lie low, and keep from angering these men further."

Boom!

Just as Spock's words finished, part of the shed exploded, blowing shards of metal and chipped paint into the small building, driving McCoy and Spock to the floor.

The door had been blown open!

Chapter 11

When the acrid, choking smoke began to billow out the smashed shed door, McCoy managed to catch a gasp of fresh air. Crouched close to the floor, he could scarcely see a thing. Greenish-brown smoke puffed around him, piling out the door.

"What happened?" he gasped. "Did they throw a bomb?"

Two long-boned hands appeared out of the smoke and coiled around McCoy's arm, then hauled him to his feet. Spock—

"This way, Doctor." The Vulcan's velvet voice came through the smoke as if part of it.

McCoy crammed his eyes shut against the stinging chemical smoke. "Did they try to kill us? Who blew up the door?"

"I did." Jimmy Kirk appeared just ahead of them at

the shed's mutilated doorway and stepped out into the crisp night air. "I used the cleaning fluids in there and blew the lock."

"You blew it, all right!" McCoy stumbled against the outer wall and coughed. "Why did you do that?"

"We've tried to beat them by being decent, logical, and predictable," Jimmy said. "It hasn't worked. I decided I should do what you said. I should be unpredictable."

"Oh, perfect! When they find us, they're going to predict us right over the nearest cliff! Don't inhale this stuff. You either, Ensign—much as you might not want to admit it, Vulcans are as mortal as the rest of us. Move away from the shed."

As the cloud dissolved in the open air, Spock said, "Take cover. They may have heard the explosion. This way."

They ran across a slab of open courtyard to a place behind a long warehouse of some kind. Once under cover of the shadows, they ducked between the warehouse and the struts of a water tower.

"I thought you always follow orders, Cadet," Spock said. "I don't recall ordering an escape attempt."

Jimmy glanced at McCoy, then back at Spock. "The situation changed, sir. I adjusted. Are you going to put me on report?"

Perplexed, yet somehow enheartened by the younger fellow, Spock gazed back at him with a twinkle in his small black eyes. "Though I'm not ready to believe that logic cannot fit every situation, your actions have given us options. I appreciate that outcome. You acted appropriately."

Jimmy blinked at him a few times. "Thank you."

"Well, team," McCoy began as he pushed between them, "now we have to decide what to do. Do we head for the hills? Do we try to make it back to the *Spitfire* and beat it out of here?"

"I would prefer to attempt contacting Starfleet again," Spock said. "In order to do that, we must shut down the damping field put off by their tractor beam."

Jimmy nodded. "Before we can take off in the *Spitfire,* we have to knock out the tractor complex anyway. And I want it knocked out just to make sure these people can't do this to anybody else. I wouldn't feel good about leaving the planet without taking away their ability to kidnap others."

"That," Spock had to admit, *"is* logical." He stepped closer to the cadet. "You seem to have a talent for understanding these men's motivations. Do any of your 'books' suggest a course of action?"

The reference to Jimmy's little old-fashioned library back in the *Spitfire* seemed to have an effect on the cadet. With the decision handed to him so openly, Jimmy balked at taking charge of whatever came next. He twitched a bit, flexed his fists open and closed, narrowed his eyes to a catlike glare, and pressed his lips flat.

"I think," he ultimately said, "we should get ahead of the bad guys and stay there."

"We can't beat those men!" McCoy exclaimed. "They've got rifles! And they outnumber us! We can't overpower them!"

"You don't have to overpower people bigger than you. You just have to surprise them. We can outsmart them."

"How? What can we do that they won't expect?"

"We've already started. We're out."

Spock gazed at the young man, but didn't say anything.

After glancing around the complex, Jimmy decided, "I think we should go on a series of hit-and-run raids. We should make this outpost as useless to them as we can. We'll have to improvise some weapons out of available material. If I can find a computer terminal, you might be able to use it to effect shutdown of some parts of the station. Maybe even the tractor beam."

"The tractor beam mainframe is inside the building these men are using as a headquarters," Spock said.

McCoy faced him. "How do you know that?"

"I saw them when they brought us to the shed."

Jimmy Kirk seized on that idea. "If we can get them to evacuate that building, can you manipulate the computer?"

"Of course," Spock said blandly. "I could encrypt the shutdown order and—"

"Great!" Cooking with excitement now, Jimmy snapped his fingers. "If I can find some medical supplies, or even the right combination of chemicals, maybe McCoy can figure out a way to tranquilize these men— gas them or make them itch—something like that. Stay here for a minute or two, and I'll make a quick run around and see what I can pick up."

"Very well," Spock told him. "You have five minutes."

"Aye aye, sir!" More comfortable with having his ideas treated as orders, Jimmy melted off into the darkness.

Aware of the crunch of gravel under his feet, McCoy came close enough to Spock to be heard at a whisper.

"Has your computer brain lost some of its circuits?" he asked. "This is incredibly risky! He's just a first-year cadet! He hasn't been anywhere except inside the pages of those books. He's barely been in the Academy long enough to know his way from the Jefferson Rose Garden to the girls' dorm!"

Suddenly several men came charging down the middle of the courtyard toward the thread of smoke still rising from the janitor's shed. Spock motioned McCoy back. The two of them sank into the shadows.

"The cadet has an intuition about the weakness of his enemies," Spock went on quietly. "He also understands how to use the skills of the people around him—at the moment, you and me. There is a certain roguish logic about his methods, and he does eventually succeed. That should not be ignored."

"I think you're reading too much sense into this horse-play," McCoy complained. "He might just be running on luck. Whether it's good or bad, who can tell?"

"I do not believe in luck. After we damage the complex, we'll confiscate one of their runabouts and escape the planet. Until then, we shall attempt Cadet Kirk's mischief, and hope it works."

McCoy pulled at Spock's arm as the Vulcan peeked around the corner of the warehouse at the men who were now looking for them. "And if it doesn't?"

"If it doesn't," Spock echoed, "those men will kill us."

"I want those Starfleet kids found, Zenoviev. Take your Klingon lapdog and find them!"

"What do you think we're doing, Joe? We already looked in ten buildings. Ten! And you know what? They're all getting cold! It's freezin' in every building!"

"I know it's freezing. We're *in* one of the buildings. What does this look like—a church?"

"I wish it was a church. Then we'd have some candles."

"You don't get it, do you?" Joe swingle clamped his arm around his skinny chest and tried to keep warm. "There's some kind of breakdown in the atmospheric control system for the complex. Go find the main furnace and air-conditioning control and fix it!"

"Okay, Joe." Zenoviev started to turn toward the door, but then he paused. His wide face worked with confusion. "Uh . . . I thought you wanted me to look for those cadets first. . . ."

Swingle squinted at his big stooge. "You are *truly* a hammerhead. Do one thing, and tell Klaag do the other thing! Can't you even think of that? Do I have to give every little order specifically? Do I have to tell you when to breathe in and out? I don't care who does what! Just get it done! Get out! Go!"

Zenoviev hulked out of the building, his breath going before him in chilled puffs. Swingle knew he would find that gargoyle Klaag, and the two of them would argue for twenty minutes about which one would do which job. Idiots. Morons. Hammerheads.

As he tried to keep warm in the frigid building, he felt the gazes of Crawler and Bonyor. Irwin and Hovitch were still out searching for the little rats who had wrecked the plan.

Bonyor looked at his bulky tricorder, his pride and

joy, and said, "It's ten degrees colder than it was five minutes ago. We're down to twenty degrees Fahrenheit. It's gonna start snowing in here in a minute. We're going to have to leave the building."

"This is where the computer complex is, you gas pellet!"

"I know, Joc, but we can't just stay in here and turn into Popsicles! Can't we track down the air-conditioning malfunction and fix it? It's got to be in the coolant lines!"

"Fine! We'll leave long enough for you to find the problem and kill it. Go on! Head for the door!" Swingle ranted as his men flinched and moved toward the door. "It was perfectly simple. Rig a tractor beam, pluck off Richard Daystrom and his driver, put a knife to the driver's throat to make Daystrom give up his new computer program, then kill the driver and ransom Daystrom back to Starfleet. The Klingons get their credits, I get my cut, and it's all over! Where does it say that three junior jockeys get to come in and blow everything! Three inexperienced, glossy-cheeked idiot cadets, and they're blowing everything!"

On the way to the door, he grabbed Crawler by the collar.

"Musclehead, you get out of here and blanket the area with infrared sensors. Track down any movement at all. If a mouse moves out of its knothole, I want to know about it. I'm gonna send those cadets back to Starfleet in a sealed bag!"

Chapter
12

"They're leaving! They're evacuating the warehouse!"

McCoy's fingers were almost numb from clinging to the high windowsill. He stood on his toes, on top of a crate full of granular fertilizer, and watched as Swingle and two more of his men burst out of the warehouse across the courtyard.

He jumped down from the crate. "You did it, Spock!"

"Of course," the Vulcan said coolly. He withdrew his delicate hands from the air-conditioning controls mounted inside this narrow tower. "The temperature in the buildings will go as low as five degrees Fahrenheit, depending upon the height of the ceilings. I've also redirected the coolant damage sensors, so they will be unable to find where the problem is. At least, not right away."

"I hope to give them too much to think about," Jimmy Kirk said. He jumped up on the crate and clawed his way to the window to make sure McCoy was right. "I suggest we get in there and get to the computer before they figure out what we're up to."

McCoy scooped up the box of chemical supplies Cadet Kirk had rounded up, and rushed out the tower door behind Spock. The cadet was already halfway across the dark courtyard.

In a few hours, it would be morning and they wouldn't be able to sneak about so easily. Or their luck, the thing Ensign Spock didn't believe in, would just plain run out.

The inside of the warehouse was crisp and frosty, like walking outside during a Minnesota winter. Instead, they were going inside. It felt very strange to go from the comfortable courtyard into a building, and be suddenly so cold.

In a way, the cold was a victory. And it was on their side.

"Do you know what to do?" Jimmy Kirk asked McCoy.

McCoy put the box of chemicals on a desk and said, "Does sulfur stink?"

The cadet swung to Spock. "The computer is over there."

Spock went to the main computer terminal. In seconds the screen was jumping with information. As McCoy hurried with his chemical bottles, he glanced up now and then to see numbers and diagrams running across the screen.

"Remarkable . . ." Spock gazed in awe at what he saw. The screen flickered in his ink-drop eyes. "This complex is magnificent. Fabulous power usage, detailed programming . . . the huge energy required to equalize

rainfall, the efficiency of climate control—I've never seen anything so cleverly organized."

McCoy leaned toward Cadet Kirk. "I think he's in love."

The cadet took one step—only one—toward Spock. "Sir . . ."

The screen flipped again. Spock studied it. "I see why they selected this planet for this experiment. There is moderate energy in the natural system here. Weather control is much more difficult when there is too much natural energy in the system."

"Sir . . ."

"For instance, heating something up is much easier than to cool it down. The manipulation of conditions is quite complex. Warming appropriate air masses by satellites, cooling others . . . causing wind that moves air masses to certain areas . . ."

"Sir, if you don't mind—"

"Applying solar heat to bodies of water to create moisture—water absorbs huge amounts of energy when it evaporates. This alone adds tremendous energy to the ecosystem—"

"Sir!"

Spock looked up. "Are you trying to say something, Cadet?"

McCoy shook a chemical burn from his finger and said, "He's trying to tell you to shut up! We've got things to do!"

Raising his eyebrow, Spock held Jimmy with a glare. "Is that what you're saying, Cadet?"

"No, sir!" Cadet Kirk blurted. "I would never say that to a senior officer!"

"But that's what he meant," McCoy insisted. "Get on with the tractor beam, would you? I'm almost finished with these grenades. Just shut it down before Swingle and his dingoes come back."

"I *have* been working on the tractor beam," Spock said, with a smile behind his eyes. "I can shut it down, but not disable it. To keep it down, the power must be cut. The subsystems transmitter must be disabled at the source. It is located in . . . Building D, diagonally across the courtyard and behind the greenhouse."

"I'll go," Cadet Kirk volunteered instantly.

"You'll need help." Spock started to get up.

"No, no . . ." Wiping chemicals from his hands, McCoy waved him back into his seat. "You keep shutting things down. And don't forget to locate those two runabouts so we can steal one and get out of here. I'll help him."

"Agreed."

"What if we can't get it to shut down?" McCoy asked as they headed for the door.

Jimmy Kirk cast back, "Then we'll blow it up."

And McCoy dashed out of the big, cold building, seeing his breath go before him in frosty funnels. Again he was following the impetuous young cadet who really hated to lose. In spite of his shorter stature and compact frame, Jimmy was a fast runner. McCoy stifled an urge to yell, "Wait up!"

But that would attract a little attention, wouldn't it?

He followed Jimmy as they skirted the edge of the courtyard, never running out into the open except to rush between the blocky buildings. The light of three moons cast a witchly glow on the courtyard's slate floor.

In the bizarre planetary night of this world, McCoy felt very alone.

But Swingle and his handful of criminals were out here too.

Looking for us. And when they find us . . .

He shimmied between awning braces to where Jimmy Kirk was peeking into a window. This must be Building D.

"There's somebody in there," the cadet whispered. "Wait here. I'll take care of it."

"But . . ." McCoy didn't know what he was about to say. They had to get in there and shut down the power source for the tractor beam. Otherwise they wouldn't be able to leave the planet.

Leaning against the shell of the building, he could feel the coolness from inside rolling out the slightly opened window. All the buildings were like refrigerators now—virtually useless. Until now he hadn't had time to think about how scary this situation had become.

He was nervous, and getting worse. If they could only shut that tractor beam off, steal a flying craft and get out of here . . .

All at once the window exploded! Crashing glass and narrow metal struts squawked as they blew outward and drove him to the slate walkway. Then something else hit him—something big! A terrible weight slammed him all the way down and held him there. He tried to turn his head and saw a big, thick arm lying across his neck, pressing his cheek to the slate. He smelled the breath of the man lying over him, and saw a streak of red hair.

They had him!

Chapter 13

"He's got me!" McCoy shouted. "He's got me!"

"He's unconscious. Shove him off."

"What?"

"He's out. Shove him right off."

Stunned, McCoy pressed his hands and toes to the slate, heaved upward, and arched his back. The man called Zenoviev rolled off his back like a sack of sand.

"Are you hurt?" Jimmy Kirk knelt beside him.

"No . . . I don't think so . . . what've you got?"

"It's his laser rifle." Jimmy cradled the weapon and picked at its controls. "Self-defense isn't exactly your best thing at the Academy, is it, sir?"

"Why should it be! I'm a medic, not a sumo wrestler."

"Rats!" Jimmy held the weapon out. "It's got a numerical safety! We can't use it without knowing the combination!"

McCoy gestured at the unconscious man. "You mean the Jolly Red Giant here knows the numbers, and that's the only way the laser rifle can be fired?"

"That's what I mean," Jimmy said with his teeth clenched.

"So it's useless?"

"Not quite. This is what I smacked him with."

"Leave it here, then."

"Not a chance. We might be able to figure out something. If nothing else, they'll be deprived of one weapon."

"Did you shut down the tractor power?"

"Yes," Jimmy said. "We should be able to get away now."

McCoy shivered in the chilly air blowing from inside the smashed window. "Assuming we can steal one of their runabouts."

"And we'll have to destroy the other one," Jimmy said as he straightened up.

"Why?"

"To maroon those men here until we can send the authorities."

"Can't they go back and use the *Spitfire* to get away?"

Jimmy shook his head. "Nope."

"Why not?"

"Because I disabled the ignition system before I got out."

"Can't they just fix it?"

"No, sir, I removed a couple of parts and hid them."

"Good thinking."

"Thanks. We'd better get back to the warehouse before Mr. Spock turns into a really dignified ice cube."

"Or before they find him."

"Right. And what do you say we do a little damage on the way?"

"Joe! Joe, five of the buildings are on fire! I can't get the fire extinguisher system to come on!"

"And the complex automatic defenses are crashed! Joe, can you hear me?"

"Joe! Joe! Over here! There's acid spilled all over the near-space communications unit! And somebody smashed all the hand-held communicators! We got no way to talk to each other anymore!"

"Hey, Joe! Klaag says to tell you all the liquid fuel's been spilled out! Somebody punched holes in every single drum!"

"Joe, up here! The tractor's down! I can't get the beam to broadcast anymore! It's gotta be those Starfleet cadets!"

"Okay, all of you shut up for a minute!" Joe Swingle shook his hands in the air, then rubbed his short haircut. Around him, his men quit giving him all these nasty reports of things going wrong. "Crawler! What's going on up there?"

He looked up, up, up, to the top of the tractor beam emission tower they'd rigged. They had taken more than a week to rig up that tower, and now the stupid thing suddenly wasn't working.

Crawler climbed down from the beam tower, shouting all the way. "The power's cut off. Far as I can tell, everything up there is working, but there's just not any juice coming through."

The grumpy electrician jumped from the ladder to the

slate floor and lumbered to him. He wiped his hands on his legs.

"I don't know what else to do, except maybe reroute power from the main complex couplings. Depends how bad you want it."

Joe drilled him with a glare. "I want it, you moron! Without it, we're sunk like a stone!"

"Okay, Joe, okay. Lay off."

Swingle shook his head and squeezed a hand over his eyes. "Kids . . . punks . . . puppies . . . I should've drowned them when I had the chance. But nooo . . . I had to be sweet."

He opened his eyes and glanced around the complex.

"They're watching us," he crabbed. "I can feel them . . . that kid with the eyes like a vulture, looking at me. He's out here right now, trying to figure out what I'm thinking. Bonyor!"

The other man poked his head out of the conduit shed he was working in. "Yeah?"

"Have you got the North Pole turned off yet?"

"I think I can get it in ten or fifteen more minutes."

"Isn't fast enough, creep. This complex is falling down around us and you want ten more minutes?"

"Look, Joe, there are certain connections that got redirected, and they take time to track. You can do it yourself if you want to. Otherwise, get off my back!"

"Just fix it, or you won't have a back!"

"Yeah, yeah."

Everybody was acting this way. Frustrated. Mad. Grumpy. Picking at each other. They were cold, they were cheated out of their reward for kipnapping a famous scientist, and now the complex was breaking down left and right. On top of that, they hated each other anyway. Crawler was an escaped convict who couldn't stick his head up without some Starfleet bloodhound breathing down his neck. Bonyor was a liar and a thief who thought any crime was right as long as he got away with it. Klaag came from the ship of the Klingon captain they were all working for. Zenoviev, Irwin, and Hovitch were just common slugs Swingle had picked up in his travels. They were like big, dumb pets. They were all just here for the ransom money. There wasn't any loyalty.

Swingle told himself again that he didn't need them to be loyal. Just greedy.

He could deal with that. He could keep them on his leash with their own greed. They didn't care how they got whatever they got in life, and he was willing to use that.

He would've felt better about it if half the complex weren't burning down around him and the other half freezing! And on top of that, it was starting to rain.

"All right, morons. We're going to get to the main power couplings and reroute the energy back to the tractor beam. Then I'm gonna start yanking ships out of space until I get Richard Daystrom. And keep looking for those cadets! First man who finds 'em gets a bonus! Spread out! What're you waiting for?"

"Wait—we can't get back."

"Why not?"

"See that light glowing over there? That's an infrared sensor. If we move, they'll be able to see us clear as daylight."

"What can we do? We can't stay here, that's for sure!"

"No. We'll have to take the long way around, keep out of its eye. Look—there's Swingle."

In the farthest corner of the courtyard, behind a cement cistern of some kind, probably used for collecting and testing rainwater, McCoy huddled behind Jimmy Kirk. They watched the searing flames eat away at several of the buildings he and Jimmy had set on fire.

Time wasn't on their side. Soon it would be daylight—only an hour or so now. The three moons had already paled to a coy pink, and the stars were fading.

In the strange light cast by the fires, Swingle and his men cluttered the courtyard near the base of the tractor beam tower. Swingle didn't look happy. He was pacing back and forth like a tiger, his head down, his hands on his hips. Now and then he paused to shout at one of the men, pointing his finger furiously into somebody's face.

"He's mad," Jimmy said. "We're getting to him."

"I wish I knew whether that was good or bad," McCoy said. "Look at that—half the complex is burning now. You're a real troublemaker, anybody ever tell you that?"

"Plenty of people. My father, mostly."

The crackle of flames whispered softly across the courtyard. A light rain began to drizzle passively, steaming against the cold building and fizzing on the hot ones.

McCoy gazed at him. Some kids had to grow up awfully fast. He got the feeling he was crouching next to one who had done just that.

"They're moving out," Jimmy said then, pointing to the six men who were hurrying away now.

"Where would they be going?"

"Looks like they're heading for the main power generators. Why would they do that?"

"Probably trying to make their beam work again, I'd guess."

"Can they do that?"

"Don't ask *me*—I'm no Vulcan."

"Yeah," Jimmy sighed. "Speaking of Vulcans, we'd better go get Ensign Spock. He's so fascinated by those weather programs, he probably wouldn't even notice if these criminals walked right in on him. We'll get him out of there, then we can steal one of their vessels and leave the planet."

"If they get the tractor beam back up, we won't be able to go anywhere."

"Don't worry. I'm not going to let them get it back up."

"I was afraid you'd say that."

"Did you start the rain, sir?"

"Yes, I did cause the rain, Cadet." Ensign Spock pressed his spine up against the side of a building and glanced out at Atlantis Outpost's main power couplings. "I indulged a bit in the weather control systems. Truly remarkable—"

"I'm glad it's remarkable," McCoy interrupted. "When this is all over, you can come back here and tamper all you please. Create snowstorms if you want. Monsoons. Deserts. But right now, let's just concentrate on getting out of here, shall we?"

He was clutching his box of homemade chemical bombs, glad he hadn't tripped as he followed the other two all the way here on the rain-slicked slate.

Between Spock and the four fifty-foot tanklike structures that were the main power couplings, Jimmy Kirk squinted through the light rain. "They're over there. I can see them. There's Swingle on the right. We can't let them hook the power back up. We've got to blow those couplings."

"Blow them?" McCoy gulped. "How?"

As if he didn't want to admit that he had no answer, Jimmy shrugged. "There's got to be a way. Look . . . their vessels are right over there, about a hundred meters past the couplings. With your permission, sir . . ." He paused and looked at Spock.

"Go ahead with your suggestion," Spock said.

Jimmy faced them. "You two go to the vessels. One of you start the engines, the other disable the other vessel. I'll take care of the power couplings, and meet you over there."

"You'll 'take care' of the couplings?" McCoy asked suspiciously. "Dare I ask again exactly what you have in mind?"

"I don't specifically have anything in mind yet, sir," Jimmy said. "But I'm sure something'll come to me."

"That's what I'm afraid of." McCoy clutched his box. "You'd better take a couple of these with you." He handed the cadet two of the six plastic bottles. "Whatever you do, don't drop them. And don't forget to take the tops off before you throw them."

"Got it." The cadet cradled his laser rifle in one arm and the two bottles in the other. "See you in a few minutes."

"When will we know to expect you?"

"Don't worry. You'll know."

He whipped around an observation tower and disappeared.

"What did he mean by that?" McCoy asked nervously. He put the box down, handed two of the bottles to Spock, and kept the last two for himself. "How'd I get into this? I went on a simple, innocent trip to a simple innocent seminar. Nothing to it. This was supposed to be a peaceful weekend. Even boring! Where am I instead? Following a Vulcan around a foreign outpost, being chased by killers, waiting for a junior cadet to wreck a power coupling bigger than my whole hometown! Brilliant! You tell me what regulation says we should take crazy chances like this?"

Spock ducked under an awning and hurried between a pair of refrigerator units. "Emergency Action Regulation T-four slash nine, subsection twelve. 'Any Starfleet personnel exposed to threatening behavior on the parts of—' "

"I didn't really want an answer!" McCoy snapped. "Might've known you'd have one."

"Ensign, it would be wise to keep your voice down, please," Spock said. "We have to cross open ground now. Be prepared. You go first. Take the vessel on the left. Start the engines. I'll disable the other vessel. Can you comply?"

"Can I start the engines? I think so. How much do you think these men trust each other?"

"I have no idea. Ready . . . go."

They started running. As hard, as fast as they could, they charged across the slippery, wet slate of Atlantis Outpost. From behind them came a yell—somebody spotted them!

McCoy dared to glance to his right—and his foot

slipped! He skidded wildly, flailing out with one arm, and nearly dropped the bottle in that hand.

Just as he regained his balance, a laser bolt streaked across the compound and grazed a metal wall, sending sparks burning over McCoy's face and hair. He ducked, barely in time to be missed by a second bright bolt.

Spock shoved him violently aside. "Down!" the Vulcan shouted over two more bolts that whined toward them.

McCoy crouched on the open slate, knowing he was a perfect target. Above him, Spock pulled the top off one of the plastic bottles full of chemicals. He raised his right arm and drew back, then with all his strength threw the bottle.

The plastic container soared almost gracefully in an arch. Some of the contents spewed out as it tumbled in midair, but most of it stayed inside.

As three of Swingle's men ran across the slate grounds, the bottle landed perfectly in the middle of the triangle they formed.

Poof! A chemical cloud exploded between the men, dousing them with choking ammonia and sulfur vapors. They staggered away, doubled over and coughing violently. The white-and-yellow cloud spread like a living thing.

"Go!" Spock called to McCoy, and caught him by the arm.

They heard Swingle's men coughing and yelling behind them.

"More are coming!" McCoy shouted. He twisted around, popped the cap, and threw one of his own bot-

tles. He escaped just as the putrid cloud puffed up in the path of the other men chasing them.

He heard the men swearing and choking behind him as he ran through the rain. Luckily, there was just enough rain to make him—and those men—uncomfortable, but not enough to ruin the clouds of his stink bombs.

*Poof—poof—*two more stink bombs went off near the bases of the power couplings. Jimmy!

McCoy and Spock were almost to the two small runabouts, and at the last minute split up. McCoy dashed to the vessel on the left, and Spock to the one on the right.

Once inside, McCoy felt terribly alone as he picked at the controls. Could he start this vehicle? He wasn't a pilot. . . .

There it was! The ignition. He pushed it with his

thumb, and the vessel hummed to life. All the control lights and the navigational computer popped on.

McCoy slid out of the pilot's seat and rushed to the hatch. "I got it started!" he shouted.

Spock appeared in the hatch of the other vessel. "Acknowledged. This one is disabled."

The Vulcan jumped out of the little craft and peered across the compound, where laser bolts were dancing wildly near the power couplings. Someone was shouting, "No, no! No! No!"

"Sounds like Swingle," McCoy panted as he joined him. "They're not chasing us anymore—look! They're all over there, looking for Jimmy!"

"Can you see him?"

McCoy squinted through the haze of rain. "Yes! There he is! Oh, no! What's he doing? Look! He's running right in front of the power couplings! He's making a target of himself!"

"No! No!" Swingle's voice carried across the grounds.

More laser bolts speared through the air between Swingle's men and the power couplings. In the flash of laser fire, McCoy could see the compact form of Jimmy Kirk dashing right across the front of the power plants.

"That's stupid!" McCoy gasped. "That crazy kid's making them shoot at him!"

"At the power couplings," Spock corrected, obviously more upset than he wanted to show. "He'll be killed. . . ."

Suddenly one of the couplings began to wheeze—the protective skin had been breached! Alarms started going off like wild animals shrieking. Then more alarms—danger bells and warnings. And a computer voice echoing all over the station:

"DANGER . . . DANGER . . . CORE BREACH . . . EXPLOSION IMMINENT . . . EVACUATE IMMEDIATELY . . . MINIMUM SAFE DISTANCE IS TWO KILOMETERS . . . DANGER . . . DANGER . . ."

Chapter
14

The tops blew right off three of the power coupling towers like volcanoes spewing hot gas. In seconds, there would be an explosion, and all the towers would ignite each other.

As the towers flamed and the alarms rang madly and the computer voice calmly instructed them to get the heck out of here, McCoy and Spock stood together, waiting anxiously and watching.

In the courtyard, sparks and bolts and clouds of stinky stuff kept them from seeing what was going on.

But they could hear—Swingle yelling in pure rage.

"You're finished, kid! It's over! Where are you, you little flathead?"

McCoy shivered at the sound of the threats.

He jumped when a form appeared nearly beside him out of the rain. Jimmy Kirk!

The cadet brushed hot sparks off his sleeves. "We're winning," he stated calmly.

"Winning?" McCoy choked. "They're madder than before!"

"Cadet," Spock began, "when did I order you to take such risks as baiting them to fire at you?"

Jimmy blinked at the Vulcan. "I thought it was implied, sir. I couldn't shoot at the couplings, so I got them to do it for me."

"Risky," Spock assessed. "But obviously effective. The tractor is down permanently. Now that you've sufficiently enraged our hosts, we should make our escape."

He gestured toward the humming vehicle on the left.

McCoy put one foot on the hatch ramp and started up, then noticed that Jimmy was gazing back across the compound instead of following him and Spock inside.

Spock doubled back to Jimmy. "Cadet?"

"Sir . . ."

"Speak up. Time is not on our side."

"Sir, I don't want to . . ."

The young man gazed longingly across the compound, no longer interested in the spewing energy field or the fires, or even the angry men rushing back and forth across the slate yard. His hands clenched tight. His lips pressed flat. He seemed almost as if he were watching something die. Something he cared about.

"Take off without me, sir," he said suddenly then.

"Without you!" McCoy pounded back down the ramp.

"I'll distract Swingle from your takeoff. I'll make sure they don't fire on you. I'll go back to the *Spitfire* and take it up so there's no chance of Swingle and his men coming after us."

"But you said it was disabled!"

"Maybe they're smart enough to enable it. We shouldn't take the chance."

"I refuse to leave you behind, Cadet," Spock proclaimed. Under his shell of Vulcan reserve he was shocked at the whole idea.

"For once, I agree!" McCoy ranted crankily.

Jimmy looked desperately from one to the other. "Sir . . . I don't want to leave . . . the . . ."

Seeing there was something else going on, Spock paused. For several seconds, in spite of the burning and exploding in the foreground, he looked only at the cadet.

"The *Spitfire,*" he said slowly. "It's your first command."

Jimmy's face flushed with color. "Yes, sir."

McCoy almost blurted how crazy that was, how stupid to be concerned about a lump of metal, a vehicle that was all the way across the compound now, parked on a dusty slab, dragged out of the valley by Swingle and his men. That didn't even have weapons!

"I agree," Spock spoke up then. "We'll take the Zodiac."

With a sigh, McCoy moaned, "Unbelievable. You're both crazy!"

"Possibly. But I understand the concept of losing a command, a ship signed to one's responsibility. I would not want a notation on my record that I let a vessel fall into hostile hands. You may stay here, if you wish, Doctor. This vehicle has a automatic takeoff and pilot program. You can make it into the spacelanes and be certain that Starfleet is notified, in case the cadet and I fail."

Spock looked at Cadet Kirk as if, for the first time,

he understood what was going on in that hot little head. Jimmy Kirk gazed back, and a tiny smile pricked at his stern lips.

There was no bucking the resolution he saw in the two powerful sets of eyes. And McCoy knew Spock was no coward.

"We'll go," he agreed. "But all of us together. As a crew."

Jimmy looked at the medic now, gratitude still flowing.

"One moment." Spock hurried inside the humming vehicle. In seconds the engines coughed, sputtered, and died. Another second later, the impulse power lines blew like popcorn. *Snap.*

Spock dodged back out the hatch. "Now!"

With Jimmy Kirk leading the way, they dodged across the Atlantis compound, this time a very familiar place. They felt a little less sticky now that Spock's rain had stopped. They saw some of Swingle's men rushing about in a panic, trying to stop the explosion that was coming, the wrecking of their power source and the end of their dirty plans.

But they never saw Single. McCoy guessed the leader would be back at the computer main, trying to get all his systems to cooperate again, maybe shut down the explosion somehow. Good luck. An energy reaction couldn't be stopped just like that.

"DANGER . . . EXPLOSION IMMINENT . . . EVACUATE IMMEDIATELY . . . MINIMUM SAFE DISTANCE IS TWO KILOMETERS . . . DANGER . . ."

The voice of the station computer echoed over and over across the open grounds. Fire flickered against the clouds.

Did Spock and Jimmy know where the *Spitfire* had been dragged? Could they find their way to it?

Choking remnants of ammonia and sulfur made him wrinkle his nose as they plunged back through the areas they had bombed with the chemical stink. Some of the smell clung to his clothing and moist hair. His lungs throbbed and his heart pounded as they ran and ran. The other two were in better physical condition, but McCoy was lanky and didn't have too much trouble keeping up.

It was a long way, though, and twice they had to duck between the buildings to escape Swingle's men, who spotted them running—

Fffffffoooooommmmmmm!

A hard slap of hot wind struck them all in the back and drove them flat to the slate. As they twisted around, they saw the power couplings blow sky-high in blinding flashes. White-hot matter phased into the pale clouds overhead. Sprouts of uncontained energy heaved upward, and outward, rolling across the burning rooftops of Atlantis Outpost.

"Hurry!" Jimmy scrambled to his feet and grabbed McCoy. "We've got to get under cover!"

"No arguments here," McCoy scratched out.

"There it is!" Jimmy pointed ahead of them.

Sure enough, sitting on a concrete slab, was the warp shuttle. Still encrusted with fire retardant, now cheesy after the rain, the compact craft was banged up and bent, but ready to fly. Jimmy had been right—the *Spitfire* was a tough customer, hard to beat.

By the time McCoy got to the small ship, Spock and

Jimmy had the hatch open and were already inside. Heart thudding, the medic plunged in and smashed his palm against the HATCH CLOSE button.

Wheezing a bit from the wrenching of the crash, the hatch squawked shut behind him, and he felt safe for the first time in hours upon hours. Now they could leave the planet! Summon help from Starfleet, and get those criminals arrested!

"Welcome aboard, Cadets."

The voice came from behind, from the storage area behind the passenger seats.

All three spun around, and found themselves staring down the barrel of the laser rifle—one that *wasn't* locked.

In fact, the barrel glowed with ready energy.

Evil-eyed and red with rage, Joe Swingle stood there wit his rifle aimed and his legs braced. There was rancorous satisfaction on his bony face.

"I figured you would come back to your little boat," he snarled. "Sure is a good thing you Academy pups are so predictable."

Chapter
15

Swingle glared at them in bald hatred.

McCoy began only now to understand just how completely the three of them had ruined this man's plans. He almost said something, but then felt a calm hand on his arm.

Jimmy Kirk was pushing him back slightly, moving forward enough that if Swingle fired that rifle, Jimmy would be the only one to get hit.

So this kid wasn't just reckless, as McCoy had let himself believe. McCoy now saw something much more in the set of Jimmy's jaw, the unblinking eyes with which he met Swingle's hate, and the poised readiness to take whatever came his way.

This was real courage. Jimmy was ready to die to protect the other two. That was a lot more than showing off or talking big.

"We've got to take off," Jimmy judged evenly, "before those explosions engulf the whole compound. If you surrender, we'll try to pick up as many of your men as we can rescue."

Despite the noble offer Swingle huffed, "Those gutless, needling slugs? I wouldn't waste my time. You just plug this tub back up, make it go, and go where I tell you. We're going to rendezvous with our friendly neighborhood Klingons."

A powerful slam rocked the shuttle, knocking McCoy to one knee, but Swingle managed to stay on his feet. Jimmy flinched as if hoping for a chance to jump the dangerous man, but there wasn't time. As if reading his mind, Spock grasped the cadet's upper arm and made sure he didn't try it.

"Enable the craft, Cadet," the Vulcan ordered. "Emergency launch. Doctor, you take the copilot's seat. I will remain here."

Clear enough. Spock didn't want McCoy left back here with Swingle while the two of them launched the ship.

McCoy wanted to argue, but didn't. If there was a scuffle, Spock would have a much better chance of winning. He did as he was told, and went into the pilot's cockpit.

"No," Swingle said. "Not him. I want Mr. Hotshot to stay right back here with me. You with the ears, you pilot the ship. Any crazy chances, and baby boy gets his hair cut the hard way."

McCoy craned to see Spock come into the cockpit and take the pilot's seat. In the passenger area, Jimmy Kirk stood with one hand on the back of a lounge, staring at Swingle.

The craft began to rumble as the engines fired up. A lifting sensation told McCoy they were taking to the atmosphere.

A tap, and Spock called to life the big main screen.

There it was—Atlantis Outpost, blowing itself to bits. Wave after wave of blustering energy washed over the *Spitfire* as Spock piloted the ship upward, off to the left, and away.

There was a terrible silence from the main compartment. Jimmy wasn't speaking to Swingle, and Swingle wasn't interested in anything a cadet had to say. The criminal just wanted to get back to the Klingons he was working for.

When they got into space, what would he do to the three of them? Certainly not keep them alive. They were of no value to him. Would they be turned over to the Klingons? Or would he just kill them all, and take over flying the shuttle himself?

Maybe he couldn't fly it. Was that possible? Maybe he didn't know how.

"Sir," Jimmy spoke then, and he was looking into the cockpit.

"Yes?" Spock answered.

"Don't forget to set the inclinometer to the port side."

McCoy watched Jimmy, and Swingle. Swingle held the rifle and peered suspiciously at them, but didn't demand that Jimmy shut up.

Then he really *didn't* know how to fly this kind of craft!

Was Jimmy making that bet?

"An excellent recommendation, Cadet," Spock said,

then glanced at McCoy. "Set the inclinometer, please, Ensign McCoy."

McCoy stared at him. He had no idea what an inclinometer was.

"Grasp that handle on your right," Spock instructed. "Hold it tightly."

There was a very slight emphasis on the word *tightly.*

McCoy grasped the handle—it was just a hand grip, not anything mechanical. "Ready," he said uncertainly.

Spock lowered his chin and fixed his eyes on his controls. "Adjusting inclination . . . now!"

The ship whined wildly and rocked up onto its left side, screaming like a vulture.

McCoy almost tumbled out of the seat onto Spock, except that he was holding on—tightly. If he hadn't been hanging on, he would've crashed headlong into Spock, and knocked Spock away from the controls.

In the main compartment, Joe Swingle howled in shock and landed on his head with one shoulder against the port side clinker plating.

Jimmy Kirk was ready. As McCoy craned to watch, the cadet now plunged straight downward to the other side of the compartment, and landed with his feet on Swingle's chest. He kicked away the laser rifle, looped his toe into the thumb grip, and flipped the rifle up into his own hands.

"Right the ship, sir!" he called.

"Acknowledged." Spock leaned into the controls. The shuttle cranked hard to starboard, wobbled like a boat, and came upright. Once again the deck was the floor instead of a wall. Dazed and confused, Swingle tried to sit up. His face was bleeding.

"McCoy!" Jimmy called.

"Coming!" McCoy unclawed his cramped hand from the thing he'd been holding and stumbled into the salon. "Yes?"

"Tie him up."

Digging into the first-aid kit, McCoy got two rubber tourniquets and used them to tie Swingle's hands behind his back.

Jimmy finally put aside the laser rifle and helped McCoy place the man between two of the lounges. Then they carefully tied him to the supports, so he couldn't even stand up.

"Good," Jimmy heaved. With a palm he pressed back his sandy hair. He pointed at Swingle's bitter face. "Sit there and shut up, mister. You're in Starfleet custody and don't forget it."

"Little blister," Swingle fumed. But there was nothing he could do.

"That's me." Jimmy straightened and took a deep breath. He looked at McCoy. "Good job."

And he held out his hand.

McCoy took the hand. "Congratulations," he offered. "You actually did it!"

Jimmy couldn't muster a grin. "I did it, but only after being caught off guard. I almost blew it, because I let him guess what I was thinking. I'm not ready to pat myself on the back. I've got to learn how to avoid letting the bad guys know what's on my mind."

"Well, don't worry," McCoy submitted. "I have a feeling you'll figure it out eventually."

With a kind of pout, Jimmy stepped over Swingle's legs and went to the cockpit.

"Good job, sir," he told Spock. "I had a feeling he didn't know how to pilot this ship and wouldn't know that we don't have an inclinometer."

"What's an inclinometer?" McCoy asked.

"It's a device used on seafaring ships. It swings back and forth and tells you how many degrees the ship is heeling over. We have artificial horizons and plane equalizers instead. I'm just glad Ensign Spock knew what I was talking about."

"I didn't," Spock admitted. "I simply surmised that you did know, and made a conclusion based on the root word 'incline.'"

"Well, whatever you did," McCoy croaked, "it worked. I'm just glad you two could understand each other."

"We did," Jimmy agreed.

Suddenly an alarm started ringing.

"What's that?" McCoy asked, and crouched between the two seats.

"Proximity alert," Jimmy told him. "There's another ship approaching."

"Magnification point seven-five," Spock said.

"Point seven-five, aye," Jimmy responded, and touched the controls.

The forward screen wobbled, hummed, and gave them a new view.

Before them moved a large creamy green ship with a long neck and two downward-hanging wings. Markings on the hull were strange, alien.

Jimmy leaned forward. "A Klingon ship!"

Chapter
16

"We can't possibly outrun them!"

Jimmy Kirk roiled with new anger at the sight of the hostile ship. One of Starfleet's oldest enemies had breached Federation space.

Perhaps it was just one crazy renegade Klingon commander doing business with Swingle, and not the whole Klingon Empire behind this, but that was enough. Three young men from the Academy in one old shuttle couldn't stand up against a full-sized enemy cruiser.

"What can we do?" McCoy choked. "They'll cut us to pieces!"

"Let's double back to the planet!" Jimmy barked. He looked desperately at Spock. "We can hide under the atmosphere! Maybe land somewhere and wait for Starfleet! We can't let them take us. Not after all this!"

"They have long-range weapons," Spock contested.

"We may not be able to outrun them back to the planet."

"It's worth a try, isn't it?"

McCoy and Spock looked at the cadet, and this time his enthusiasm caught them both.

"Yes," Spock confirmed. "It is. Coming about."

"Hold on," Jimmy said to McCoy.

"Oh, I am," the medic responded, and grasped the supports of Jimmy's seat.

The *Spitfire* whined as it was forced about in a tight arch, back toward the planet. The main screen showed the planet again, rolling before them.

"Increasing speed," Spock uttered.

Jimmy watched the secondary monitor, which still showed a picture of the approaching Klingons. "Hope it'll be enough . . . sir! I'm picking up another contact! It's another ship!"

"Not another Klingon!" McCoy gasped.

Tampering with his controls, Jimmy frowned at the sensor readouts.

"Gross tonnage . . . hull size . . . configuration . . . exhaust signature . . . sir! Sir! It's a starship! Set a new course!"

"Veering toward it!" Spock responded over the whine as he once again peeled the ship off in another direction. Even he was breathing fast. "Intercept course."

"They're hailing us!"

"On audio."

"Audio, aye."

"This is the U.S.S. Enterprise, *Captain Christopher Pike commanding. Come in, Zodiac* Spitfire."

Jimmy looked at Spock, and so did McCoy.

But Spock didn't answer the hail. He looked at the main screen, now showing a brilliant white swan-shaped form coming out of the darkness toward them.

"Well, Spock?" McCoy prodded. "Aren't you going to answer him?"

Spock hesitated another few seconds.

"No," he said. "I shall not be the one answering." He looked at Jimmy then, with a particular warmth in his reserved face. "The commander of this vessel will answer for it."

Choked up, Jimmy Kirk could barely manage to stare at him without crumbling. But he managed to keep control of himself and didn't get mushy.

He took a deep breath, a little grin pulling at his mouth, and nodded a silent thank-you.

When he could unknot his throat, he punched the comm button.

"This is Cadet James T. Kirk, pilot of the Zodiac *Spitfire*. We were yanked off course by mercenaries. We escaped and took the leader into custody. We're being pursued by a Klingon vessel. Do you read?"

"Yes, Cadet Kirk, we read you. We've warned off the Klingons and they're moving out of Federation space. They've no stomach for taking on this ship!"

That smile finally popped out on Jimmy's face. "I don't blame them, sir. She's something to see coming."

As they watched, the *Starship Enterprise* grew large on their forward screen, and larger, and larger. McCoy stared in plain shock at the size of the beautiful ship and the sparkle of sunlight on the bright white hull.

"Captain," Jimmy went on, "these men were after

Richard Daystrom. Did he make it to Colony Cambria safely?"

"Yes. Dr. Daystrom is fine. When your Zodiac disappeared, we made the connection. We picked up your mayday and have been searching for you for hours. Dr. Daystrom will be put under double guard and ferried about safely from now on. Let me offer you and your friends a peaceful tour of a very pretty ship, and dinner with me in my cabin, all right?"

"We'd love that, sir," Jimmy accepted. "Sir, you'll want to arrange to pick up the other mercenaries. They're marooned on Atlantis Outpost. And they were dealing with the commander of that Klingon ship. It was a plot to ransom Dr. Daystrom."

"Understood. We'll hand the matter over to Federation Intelligence and let them confront the Empire about this espionage."

"Thank you, sir."

"All right, Kirk, our bay is ready for you. Prepare to come aboard."

"Acknowledged." Jimmy looked at Spock.

The Vulcan touched the controls. "Beginning final approach."

Before them the bay doors of the starship's massive docking area slowly opened. Overhead, the cigar-shaped warp nacelles streaked outward behind the ship like great white wings.

"I had the opportunity to meet Captain Pike a few years ago," Spock offered. "He is an exceptional man. This should be a fascinating experience."

"This whole thing has been fascinating. They're proba-

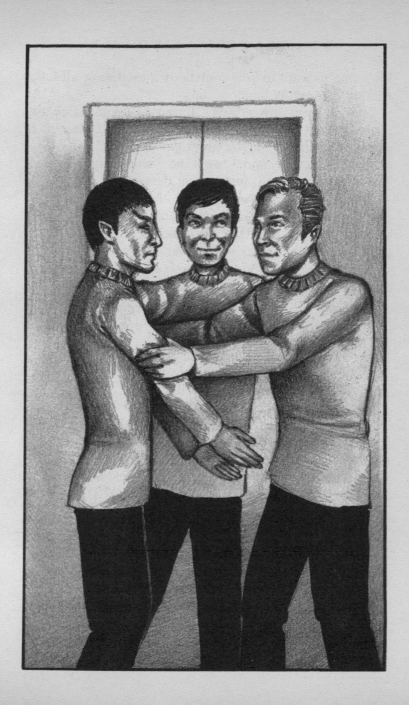

bly going to want to give somebody a medal for all this," McCoy crowed as he stood up.

"I don't want any medals," Jimmy told him. "I've gotten more out of this than I ever expected. I learned to trust my instincts. Maybe improvise a little."

"Still," McCoy said, "we'll be submitting a report. You'll get full credit, just as you deserve."

Jimmy turned toward him in the copilot's seat. "I don't want it. Please, sir . . . we acted as a crew. That's all that matters. Starfleet personnel need to look up to somebody with officer's bars, not down to somebody with cadet's slashes. Someday maybe I'll earn those bars. But for now, I just want to be part of the crew."

With new admiration, McCoy realized he shouldn't be so surprised. This kid was one step ahead of him all the way.

The cadet turned to Spock. "It's been a privilege serving with you, sir. Sorry if I caused you trouble. You'll make a good commander someday."

He offered his hand solemnly.

Spock gazed at him briefly, then took the hand. "When that day comes, Cadet, I hope you'll serve in my crew."

Jimmy Kirk tightened his grip on Spock's hand.

"Aye, sir," he declared, "I hope so too."

About the Author

DIANE CAREY is the author of over twenty novels, including twelve *Star Trek* books, two Civil War novels, and several other historical novels. She collaborates with her husband, Gregory Brodeur, who is talented in plot development and editing. The couple lives in a small historic city in the middle of Michigan with their three children.

When she's not hammering at the keyboard, Diane slips away to work as a deckhand and bosun aboard several tall ships, including the *Pride of Baltimore II,* a replica of the Baltimore clipper that helped win the War of 1812.

About the Illustrator

TODD CAMERON HAMILTON is a self-taught artist who currently lives in Kalamazoo, Michigan. He has been a professional illustrator for the past ten years, specializing in fantasy, science fiction, and horror. Todd is the current president of the Association of Science Fiction and Fantasy Artists. His original works grace many private and corporate collections. He has co-authored two novels and several short stories. When he is not drawing, painting, or writing, his interests include metalsmithing, puppetry, and teaching.

BEAM ABOARD FOR NEW ADVENTURES!

Pocket Books presents a new, illustrated series for younger readers based on the hit television show:

Young Jake Sisko is looking for friends aboard the space station. He finds Nog, a Ferengi his own age, and together they find a whole lot of trouble!

Published by Pocket Books

954-07

"There they are," Cadet Kirk said.

McCoy looked up. On the screen, inside the bright circles of the landing pad, were several men watching them come in.

"What're they holding?" he asked.

"Laser rifles, that's what!" Abruptly Cadet Kirk leaned into his controls, snapped off a couple of connections, and took the throttle in his right hand and the steering console in his left. He leaned forward, and the engines whined in response.

"Cadet!" Spock shouted. "We will overshoot the complex!"

The cadet nodded sharply. "I'll be sure to do that, sir!"

At that instant, the Atlantis complex sheared past beneath them. Instead of veering toward it, the craft muscled past, screaming and fighting against the tractor beam.

"That was not an order!" Spock reached out for the piloting controls. "Stop immediately!"

The cadet put out his own hand, just long enough to nudge Spock back. Not exactly a hit, but a firm bump. "Too late, sir!"

"Release your controls, Cadet!"

"It's too late! Everybody hang on! We're crashing!"